the Bear in the Storm

River Fork
the Bear in the Storm

J. M. Orise

Orise Designs Publishing, LLC
jm@jmorise.com

Cover design by Jo M. Orise

Illustrations by Jo M. Orise

First edition 2026

This is a work of fiction. Any references to historical events, real people, or real places are used fictitiously. Other names, places, characters, businesses, or events are products of the author's imagination. Any resemblance to actual events or places or persons, living or dead, should not be inferred, and such resemblances are entirely coincidental.

SBN: 978-1-968529-00-0 for paperback

LCCN: 2026906012 for paperback

ISBN: 978-1-968529-01-7 for e-book

LCCN: 2026906456 for e-book

First edition May 2026

Publisher:
Orise Designs Publishing L.L.C.
Owls Head, ME

https://jmorise.com
jm@jmorise.com

In memory of my mom, Orise, my dad, Red,
and my sister, Lucille.
I also dedicate this to
Tom, Jason, Gwen, and Henry,
and to my high school students who shared their grief.
My heart goes out to those mourning the death of another.
Hopefully, this story will help readers realize their lost loved ones are
still present in spirit.
Listen with your heart.
You will hear them.

Preface

J. M. Orise, a former high school teacher, tailored her lesson plans to the student age group and personal experiences.

One such lesson instructed her students to write their autobiography, with the added challenge of "Fact, Fiction or Fix-it." And they were ensured their submitted stories would be private—confined between writer and teacher.

The outcome stunned Orise. Several students mourned the loss of a parent, sibling, relative, or friend, which triggered the memory of her own mother being trapped in a house fire when Orise was five years old. That she and Lucille, her seven-year-old sister, made several unsuccessful attempts to save their mother. And that her family avoided conversations regarding the event.

The collective grief of her students and the echo of her own bereavement, was the impetus for Orise to pen her River Fork series, book 1 debut novel, <u>River Fork: The Bear in the Storm</u>.

As author of the series, she navigates the landscape of childhood grief, love, coming of age, and self-discovery through the lens of historical fantasy.

"Tears shed for another person are not a sign of weakness. They are a sign of a pure heart."

José N. Harris

Contents

River Fork
North Conway
Saco River
Uncle Sal's farm
Cave
Old Wood
Dodge Hill Rd.
Gram's farm
Magic Meadow

Saco River
Tim's camp
Cemetery
Dodge Hill Rd.
Lower Wood
Charlie's farm
Dodge Hill Rd.
Old Wood
Tim's farm
© Tom Orise 2025

Chapter 1

1956

TIM SAUNDERS POKED HIS forkful of pancake into the maple syrup river surrounding his pancake island.

"Dad? Can—" Tim glanced at Mom. "*May* I be excused from work today?"

Wesley stirred his coffee. "Why?"

"It rained lots last night. Night crawlers will be everywhere! Figured I'd dig up a mess of 'em for the next time we go fishin' at the Saco River."

"Oh, you figured we'd go fishin', huh? When?"

"Tomorrow. You promised we'd go tomorrow. You won't have to dig up any worms. *I'll* do that."

"So, a twelve year old is taking over my job? Just remember, I'm still the boss." Dad smiled, eyeing Tim over the rim of his coffee mug. "What do you think, Nel? Tim wants the day off."

Mom placed the butter dish at the center of the table. "Tim works with us every day. Boys need fun once in a while, Wes. He'll be a farmer soon enough. I vote Tim digs up all the worms he can find. But don't get any for me. I got chores and cooking to do."

"Thanks, Mom," said Tim, his voice muffled by a mouthful of pancake, and maple syrup dripping on his chin.

"Well, okay. You can take the day off. But you'll have double chores tomorrow. And you'll have to help unload the firewood I'll be cutting today with Uncle Sal. Will you be able to handle it?"

Tim wiped the syrup with his forefinger and sucked it clean with his lips.

"I can handle it. Thanks Dad. Tomorrow, I'll get up extra early, do my regular chores, help unload the firewood, and I'll even stack it for you. Promise. Then we'll go fishin'."

"Mom, can I have a sandwich and milk for lunch? I'll be back for supper time."

"May I," said Mom.

"Oh. Yeah. Sorry. May I?"

Mom packed a peanut butter and strawberry jam sandwich, poured milk in a thermos, set them next to Tim's plate, while her other hand reached up to his head, smoothing his hair, parting it *her* way.

Tim leaned a little out of Mom's reach with a smirk. "I already took care of my hair, Mom." Getting up, he wiped his sticky lips with the back of his hand and headed for the door. "Thanks for the lunch. See you later." Once in the barn, he brushed his hair with his fingers, pushing it back without a part. He preferred it *his* way.

Tim bicycled to every secret place he and Charlie Wallace knew where earthworms were sure to be found on Dodge Hill Road. A scattering of five neighboring farms dotted the eighteen miles of his road. One boy near Tim's age lived thirteen miles west of Tim's farm. Charlie lived three miles away at the east end. Although he was three years older, they had been friends since Tim could ever remember. They were like brothers and often went fishing together on the Saco.

By late afternoon, as the sun cast long shadows across the fields, Tim slipped two Maxwell House Coffee cans, heavy with damp dirt and night crawlers, into the pouch slung across his chest. He pedaled back home to the barn and placed the coffee cans and pouch on a shelf before heading to the house with his empty thermos.

He stepped up to the porch screen door, but Mom quickly engaged its hook and eye latch, preventing his entry! Her bloodshot eyes seemed to gaze beyond Tim. She stood there, rubbing her hands up and down; first her palms then the backs of her hands and her palms again, wiping them onto her badly stained apron. She repeated the motion as if unaware with her head slightly tilted to her right shoulder.

"Mom?" Tim whispered, his brow furrowed.

Straightening her stance, Mom's eyes locked with Tim's. "Go to Gram's. Now. Don't come back until I say so. You understand?"

Confused, Tim leaned forward, for the hoarseness in her voice made it difficult to hear. He nodded slightly.

Mom pivoted, walked through the kitchen, and disappeared into the living room.

Tim paused. Peered through the screen. No. He didn't understand. Something was wrong, but he sensed he shouldn't ask.

He stepped down from the porch, left the thermos on the top step, and trudged across the family's twelve acre hay field called the Magic Meadow to Mabel Hallstead's farmhouse. Everyone called her Gram.

Gram was nice. But her fourteen year old granddaughter, Roach, stuck her nose into everyone's business, and she never shut up. Her need to have the last word drove Tim crazy!

Gram opened her weather-worn screen door and greeted Tim. Did she expect him? Did she know why Mom sent him here? Why didn't he ask Mom to explain why he had to go to Gram's and not come back until she said so?

The smell of hot biscuits prompted a peek from Tim to Gram's oil-fired kitchen stove. On her enameled-top table sat a heap of kneaded bread dough. Tim noticed the table's second leaf pulled out. Did Gram make room for him to sit because she knew he was coming?

Roach was nowhere in sight. Tim smiled at that welcome relief.

"Have a seat. Can I offer you milk an' a hot biscuit?" said Gram.

"No, thanks, Gram."

"You sure? Fresh from the oven."

He shook his head. "Why did Mom send me here? Is-is she angry? At me?"

"Oh, don't think that. Sit here a while. She'll let us know what to do."

"Why?"

"Have a bite? Hot biscuit with jam? Roachelle's favorite."

Tim slowly turned in his chair, surveying the kitchen, expecting Roach behind him. "Where is she?"

"Out working. Mostly playing, I suspect. Hard to predict Roachelle. Even after I tell her what to do." Gram smiled and shook her head.

In the distance, through the kitchen window's sheer curtains, Tim spotted Uncle Sal moving Dad's truck from the house and parking it near the barn. Mom stepped out to the porch railing. Pointing to the screen door, she signaled Uncle Sal to hurry back, paused for a quick glance toward Gram's, and stepped back inside.

They're in a hurry. For what? Where's Dad? His truck is there, so he has to be home.

Soon, a sheriff's car and a white station wagon, each with lights flashing, drove into Tim's driveway. The white wagon drove up close to the porch where Dad's truck had been, and Uncle Sal rushed out the screen door to greet the driver.

Tim jumped from his chair, heading toward Gram's door.

Gram's firm voice stopped him. "Stay here! Your mom will let you know when to go. This is business for grownups. You'll be okay here."

"But that's a sheriff. Why is that station wagon there with them lights flashing? Those men with Uncle Sal— What's going on?"

"That's an ambulance. You never seen one before?" said Roach, walking through the kitchen's back entry with a basket of fresh lettuce.

Tim spun around, facing her. "No."

"They pick up—"

"Someone got hurt," said Gram.

"Hurt? Who?" said Tim, looking from the window to Gram and back to the window. He headed for the screen door.

Gram stepped up to Tim. "Just relax. Your mom will call. Everything will work out." She cradled his elbow in her hand and patted his hair back with her other hand. Her touch calmed him. Somewhat. It stopped him from leaving.

Mom's words, "Don't come back until I say so," echoed in Tim's head.

Frowning, he walked to the door and pressed his forehead into the screening. He watched. Minutes passed. There were two deputy sheriffs. One went inside; the other stayed by the car. What were they doing? Out of respect for Mom's wishes, he fought the urge to run home.

Uncle Sal stepped out from the kitchen, kept the porch door open for the two ambulance men who hurriedly carried someone on a stretcher from the house. A deputy followed. Mom stepped out, but stayed on the porch. Uncle Sal put his arm around her shoulders, speaking to her. Her head leaned against his chest for a few seconds.

"Dad? What's happening?" said Tim with a whimper.

Roach slipped her hand into Tim's, but he immediately pulled his hand free, flung the screen door open, bolted onto the porch, jumped from the top step, and ran.

The brilliant red lights whirled. Round and round. Why didn't they turn them off?

The deputy rushed from the porch and opened the back door to the ambulance. The men pushed the stretcher inside. One man jumped in with the stretcher, the deputy shut the door, and the other man slipped into the driver's seat, backed the vehicle, turned it around, and drove back out.

"Wait! Wait for me!" yelled Tim.

The ambulance switched on its siren.

"Stop! Wait!" Tim's heart raced, his breath grew short. Tears blurred his vision. He focused on the sheriff's and the ambulance's whirling lights as the vehicles sped from the gravel drive. Why didn't they turn off the lights?

"No!" He waved his arms to catch their attention. "Turn off those stupid lights. Bring him back! Bring Dad back!"

"Tim!" Mom yelled from the bottom porch step.

Uncle Sal ran up to Tim and grabbed his arm to stop him.

"Let go. Let go. I want to see Dad." Tim punched his uncle's arm with his fist. He spun around and elbowed him at the waist. Once free, he ran, following the siren's wail, which had turned onto Dodge Hill Road.

He reached the turn at the end of his drive, but the ambulance was gone.

So was Dad!

Chapter 2

1957

Summer temperatures grew intolerable. High humidity and lack of rain made farming a challenge. Gardens, cornfields, and hayfields wilted.

Local folks expected the hot weather to give way to thunderstorms. In the past, after similar dry spells, River Fork experienced horrendous storms. Sometimes lightning came from nowhere. One strike could explode a tree into splinters, or leave an angry scar where the sap boiled deep inside its trunk. However, according to Dad, a storm's rain also replenishes farmland and the Saco River.

Tim helped Mom tend the garden and milk Suzie, their Holstein, who produced ten quarts of milk every day, which Mom sold, along with eggs, at River Fork's Village Green, and to her regular customers who came to purchase at the farm.

Tim filtered the milk into galvanized milk cans and carted them to the milk house. He shoveled manure from the barn stall and spread new hay to freshen it, then he put all the garden tools away while Mom fed Suzie and the chickens.

After three weeks of farm chores in ninety-eight to one hundred degree temperatures, Tim longed for a trip to the Saco River. And his mind wandered to his upcoming birthday—July 19th. He'd be thirteen.

I'll be older, taller. Not a little kid anymore. Tim smiled at the thought.

With chores finished, he hurried back to the house, scrubbed his hands and face, and threw the towel into the kitchen sink. According to the clock, supper was yet two hours away.

Tim ran out the door and down the driveway, calling over his shoulder, "Mom! Gonna visit Dad. Be back later."

"No! You don't have time. I need you here to—"

Her son was out of earshot.

The day's chores had drained Nel's energy and patience. Still, her lips curved upward in a faint smile. She shook her head.

Tim disappeared over the upper ridge, grumbling, "I'll go if I want. She can't stop me."

He ran across the farm's field to the outer edge of the family forest, called the Old Wood. There he took a shortcut through the woods, jogging and jumping over branches, rocks, and fallen tree limbs. From under the canopy of trees, where shade provided the welcomed cooler air, he caught a glimpse of the late afternoon sky.

He never feared the woods. Dad had said, "Because you live near a forest and a river, you'll never be hungry. If you get lost, pay attention to the animals. Follow them, they'll lead you to the river. From there, follow the river upstream to Uncle Sal's." He taught Tim how to identify north by the moss growth on the north side of tree trunks and lichen forming on the north side of boulders. The moss and lichen served as natural compasses.

His feet pounded the crushed stones of the narrow gravel road winding through the Old Wood. He stopped to catch his breath at a fence that appeared on the right. The fence's structure consisted of three lengthy horizontal black iron pipes. The pipes ran through rough-cut holes in the rectangular granite posts planted deep into the ground at four-foot intervals. The entry gate was closed. Locked. Touching his forehead on one of the iron pipes, Tim cooled his sweaty brow. Once recovered, he slipped through between the pipes, made his way along a narrow path and sat in his usual spot, in the shade of a weathered sugar-maple. Its leaves hung motionless in the evening's still, humid air.

He leaned against the trunk's rough bark and patted the grass on which he sat. Plucking a wide blade of grass, he placed it flat along the edge of his thumbs, brought his hands to his mouth, and blew between his thumbs. "Brweeeee. Brweeeeeeee." Whenever he and Dad got separated in the woods, they had used grass whistles to find each other. Now, he did this whenever he visited Dad—greeting him.

He looked up. "Hello Dad. Wanted to bring you something. Didn't have time, though. Sorry. Mom tried to stop me. So I ran off quick. Gotta get back for supper to help with chores before dark."

Tim gazed at the surrounding mountains. River Fork consisted of farming and logging country. The land rolled up and down like an ocean bounded by mountains. Remnants of ancient volcanoes had formed a ring-dike, flanking the town from the west. Mount Washington towered on the Northern horizon.

The Saco River lay five miles from the Saunders' farm, as the crow flies. The drive to town was fifteen miles. No shortcuts.

Generations of Saunders had lived in River Fork. First, Great Grandfather Wesley, then Grandfather Elmer, and finally, his dad, Wesley. Each generation updated and improved the farm to suit its needs. Though Tim lived in the same farmhouse, life on the farm was different now.

"I miss you a whole lot. Wish you'd come back home. Mom does too. I can see it in her eyes. But she don't talk about you.

"She been talking to Uncle Sal about moving away to the city. Boston. You ever been there? I don't want to go. I don't want to move away with Mom and leave you here by yourself. What will I do in Boston? Charlie said he's been there. It's a giant city in Massachusetts. Not like River Fork, where everybody knows everybody else."

Tim closed his eyes, his throat knotted. Noticing the position of the sun, he said, "I gotta go. Don't worry, I'll be back tomorrow." He got up and, like he always did after each visit, traced his fingers along the etched marks spelling his dad's name, Wesley T. Saunders, 1919-1956.

Tim blinked furiously, willing the threat of tears away. "Babies cry. People think I'm still a baby. I don't want to cry anymore, Dad. When will Mom, Uncle Sal, and everyone else realize I'm nearly a grown-up?"

Tim walked the perimeter of the fence, reading names from the other headstones. There were lots of Civil War and WWII veterans. Little flags rose through the soil, saluting at odd angles. And there were babies, boys, girls, wives, husbands. And Dad.

Leaning against the fence, staring at Dad's headstone, Tim remembered a story Dad once told him about a bear. Tiny Bear. It had rescued Dad and Uncle Sal when they were nine and ten years old. Dad said the bear had powers. Were the powers magical? If so, why hadn't it rescued Dad last summer?

Tim's eyes watered. "Dang! I'm not gonna cry. Not any more.

"Bear! Bring Dad back!"

An unexpected breeze rustled the tall grass and weeds on Dad's grave. The other graves, however, lay motionless, as did the maple tree. Not one leaf or branch moved, but the leg of Tim's dungarees gave a sudden flutter at his shin. Did something travel by him? He shook his head. Had to be a breeze predicting a cooler day for tomorrow. That would make chores around the farm easier for him and Mom.

"River Fork could sure use a cool breeze for a change," said Tim, crossing his fingers to make it so.

He walked back home, remembering the times he'd spent with Dad. Happier times. Tim loved the farm, his friends, school, and the countryside. He didn't want to live in Boston. If Dad was alive, they would live in River Fork forever.

With clenched fists deep in his pockets, he kicked hard at a stone on the gravel roadway. "It ain't fair that you're gone, and now we have to leave. I want you back home with me. With Mom."

Tim turned and stared at the cemetery. Dad's granite headstone stood barely visible now among the multitude of other older moss-covered headstones. Dad's stone, no longer clean and new, would soon resemble the others. Kinda like disappearing.

Tim shut his eyes for a few seconds, then bolted down the road, blurred by his tears. A large red sun slowly stained the horizon, and inch by inch, melted behind a far ridge of the New Hampshire mountains.

That evening, at bedtime, Tim punched his pillow into place. Dressed in his pajamas, he stood barefoot with arms raised and dropped forward onto his old cotton mattress. The bed frame groaned, the springs creaked and popped. The iron-pipe bed hit the side wall with a thud.

He yanked the beaded chain anchored from his headboard to the ceiling light's pull-chain to switch off the light.

Staring at the darkened ceiling, he wished he could go back in time. Go back an entire year. He'd grab Dad's hand and never let it go. He'd bring him home where he belonged. But that would be impossible. Or would it?

Unable to sleep, he pulled the blankets over his face. His nostrils flared, sucking in the fresh smell of clean sheets. Everything Mom washed smelled fresh, like the woods he often tramped through with his friend Charlie.

Mom walked upstairs to her bedroom, and Tim heard drawers opening and closing—she seemed busy moving things about.

Mom's fussing around in her bedroom. Used to be Dad's room, too. What's she doing? Whispering to herself? Moving things around? She leaves the hall light on most nights. Is she scared of the dark, too? Like me?

Peeking from under his blanket-cavern, he watched the light creeping in under his door. After a long spell, Mom quieted, and the hall light flickered out. She had settled for the night.

Finally!

He mumbled Mom's words, "Turn off your light. Don't fret about the dark. You'll be fine." What did she know about his room? That it would be fine?

Near his nightstand, beneath his window, stood that *door*.

The door.

The *attic* door.

When Tim was four, Dad warned him to not open that door. Why? Tim wondered if anything lived behind that door. Ghosts? Would they come into his room? At night?

When Tim was six, J. J. Jones, a classmate, talked about monsters and ghosts. Said they came around after dark and hid under beds. Sometimes they dragged kids off, never to be found again. Or they just hid under beds. Tim was okay if they stayed under there and were quiet. Another time, J. J. had snatched several comic books from his older brother and shared them with Tim. They had stories and pictures of vampires. Ever since then, going to the bathroom downstairs in the middle of the night was no longer an option for Tim. He waited till morning.

At the edge of sleep, a noise startled him awake.

There's that running, scratching noise again! Back and forth, back and forth. In the attic on my ceiling. Has to be a mouse.

The minutes ticked away on Dad's Big Ben alarm clock, sitting on Tim's nightstand. After hundreds of tick-tock-ticks, Tim fell asleep.

Most nights, he dreamed of things he and Dad had done together. But one particular dream haunted him—often. He dreamed it again tonight.

Tim and Dad sat on a fallen tree at the Saco River. The water roared as it flowed. Dad stood, pointed to the river, and spoke. But Tim couldn't hear. Before he could ask what he'd said, Dad disappeared into the shadows of the Lower Wood forest at the edge of the Saco.

Tim ran to catch up, but he sank ankle deep into the muddy marsh. Trees fell around him. The river rose over its banks. Suddenly, he was swimming, but in the wrong direction! Unable to turn back, the river swept him away. No matter how quick his strokes were, he couldn't swim ashore. He yelled, "Dad! Come back! Help me!"

Startled awake by his nightmare, Tim found himself soaked with perspiration. Pulling off his pajama top, he threw it to the foot of the bed and kicked his blankets to the floor.

"Why did you leave me in the river?" he whispered. "Come back. Tell me what you said!"

As he lay motionless, a tear trickled into his ear; another created a damp spot on his pillow. Wiping the tears, he rolled onto his stomach and buried his head under the pillow.

"I don't want to dream anymore, Dad! I just want *you* to come back. Where you belong. With me. With Mom. I want to stay in River Fork. Make Mom change her mind. Make her want to stay here. With me. With you."

Chapter 3

TIM MAKES A PLAN

AT DAWN, TIM AWOKE, squinting through his red eyelashes as the sunlight nudged its way around the edges of the dark green window shade; slowly lighting up his room. He thought about Dad's stories. The last story involved a bear. Tiny Bear. The tiniest bear in the world. If you were in trouble, you could ask for help. But you had to believe in the bear. If you truly believed, it would help you.

Dad's brother, Uncle Sal Saunders, had broken his ankle when they were kids. They had been out hiking together. The bear helped the brothers get home. And Dad became friends with the bear. Dad said so.

If it rescued Dad and Uncle Sal once with its magical powers, maybe it could bring Dad back home again. I need to find the bear. Now! But where is he?

Could Uncle Sal help find it? No, *he* wouldn't help. He'd stopped Tim from seeing Dad when the ambulance came last year. Besides, Uncle Sal didn't even like Tim. The feeling was mutual.

Watching the golden glow of morning sunlight creeping into his room, Tim analyzed the story of the bear.

It makes no sense. The tiniest bear in the world? Is it a made-up story? Could be. But Dad wouldn't lie. Grandfather Elmer mentioned it once. He wouldn't lie either. It has to be true! The bear must have magical powers. If Grandfather knew about Tiny Bear, that bear's been around for a long time. Do bears grow old like people do?

He planned to ask Dad about the bear the next time they went camping. But he never got the chance. Why hadn't he asked more questions when he had the chance?

If the bear was Dad's friend, then why didn't it help Dad last summer?

It ain't fair—Dad being gone. I gotta find that bear. Tell him a thing or two.

"You bring Dad back! You hear me, Bear?" said Tim.

A sudden puff of wind blew the window shade into the room, flipping and rolling it upward with a loud snap. Tim sat up straight, watching. The shade flipped round and round atop the window, then slipped off its bracket. It fell, knocking Tim's alarm clock under his bed with a crash and a ding. The shade's metal end dented the linoleum floor with a thud. The opposite end struck the attic door, pushing it ajar.

Not sure what lurked in the attic, Tim dove off the bed, caught and slammed the door shut. He crawled under his bed, ignored the old toys, dirty socks, dungarees, comic books, and other treasures he'd found in the woods, littering the floor, and retrieved his clock.

Setting the clock on his nightstand, he noticed it no longer ticked. The wing nut refused to wind. The other buttons twirled the hour and minute hands. Now, unable to set the button to ring an alarm, he couldn't test the clock. It no longer worked. Tim shook it. Nothing happened. He tossed it up and caught it. Nothing. He slammed it onto his bed. Nothing.

His eyebrows knitted tight. Dad's Big Ben died.

Suddenly, a smile spread across Tim's face as he returned the clock to the nightstand

"Dad'll fix it when he gets back. Promise me you'll do that, Dad," said Tim.

Outside his window, the rising sun had grown larger and redder. Tim's shoulders slumped. He left his bedroom and mumbled, "Ah, gee. Another hot, muggy day for farming."

The next evening, out on the front porch, Mom took a seat on the metal glider and retrieved a spool of white thread and a sewing needle from her mending basket. Tim sat next to her. Worn socks lay in a pile between them. Each sock had a hole in the toe or the heel. After threading the needle, she inserted a wooden darning egg into a sock and began mending its hole from edge to edge, weaving it shut with thread. Tim watched the hole get smaller and smaller, and gone. The stitching became solid fabric, like the rest of the sock.

Like...magic? Yeah. Like magic. Mom made something that disappeared come back. Just like I want to make Dad come back. If she can do that, why can't a magical bear do that? I need a plan to find the bear.

Staring at the Old Wood marking the edge of the Saunders field, then beyond to the distant mountains to the North and West, he wondered how and where he might find the bear? Caves were logical. That's where they hibernated. After hibernation, did they return at night to sleep in the same cave? The way he returned to his room to sleep?

How small was tiny? Hopefully, nobody had stepped on the bear. He imagined it crushed into the forest trail. That would be a disaster for Tim. But mostly for the bear. Maybe Charlie could help. He was older than Tim. And smart.

Charlie liked to tease. "With all that red hair and freckles, you look like a short red tomata, Tomata Head."

At five years, Tim had replied, "*You're a big* red tomata yourself."

Charlie laughed. "No, I'm not. My hair ain't red and my skin is black. I don't get all rosy. Ain't possible." Tim grinned at the memory.

"Mom. Can I go to Charlie's?"

"May I?" said Mom.

"What?"

"May I?"

"Oh. Yeah. May I?"

"Say 'Yes'."

"Yes, what?" Tim frowned as he walked into the kitchen for a glass of water.

"Please don't keep saying 'Yeah.' The word is 'Yes.'"

"Okay. May I go to Charlie's?"

"Yes, you may go. I'll have supper ready by six."

"Thanks, Mom."

"Say hello to Mrs. Wallace and Charlie for me."

Mrs. Lila Wallace directed Tim to the back of the barn where Charlie worked under the hood of his dad's 1931 Ford pickup. The fenders sported dents and dings; the once red paint had turned dull and worn. Rust had chewed at parts of the body and the underside. Charlie's dad, Spencer, had repaired a hole in the cab floor with a cedar board and a couple of old steel carriage bolts. Although the truck ran okay, it often needed tinkering.

A dozen or more feral cats roamed the barn. Two of them, feet and tails dangling from the cross timber above where Charlie worked, warily eyed Tim's approach.

"Hello Tomata. What's up?" said Charlie.

"Thinking about an overnight camp-out to explore our secret cave. What do you say! Wanna go?"

"Hm-m. Yeah. But first I gotta get this truck running again. I got lots of chores to do. Plus the vegetable stand needs filling for when folks come by," said Charlie without looking out from under the hood.

"Can I help ya with the truck?"

"Dunno. It's tough work for a little guy." Charlie pulled hard at the box wrench. "Dang it. Thing won't budge." He pulled once more with greater effort. The nut refused to turn. "Little oil will do the trick. It'll come out." He tossed his wrench into a large wooden tool tray, grabbed his oil-stained rag, and wiped his greasy hands.

"Maybe some other time, Tomata."

"It's so hot. I want to go now. I've got it all figured out. We'll be getting two things done at the same time."

"What two things?"

"Going on the Saco to explore the cave, for one."

"Could use a break from this awful heat. And hungry mosquitoes," said Charlie.

"Great! How about—"

"What's the second thing?"

"Oh. We need to find something. Well, *I* need to. And you're gonna help. Cause you're good at figuring out stuff."

"Find what?"

"I can't tell you just now. It's a secret. I'll let you know when we go."

"Mm-mm. Top secret? No worry, cats won't tell. But if we had pigs around—"

"They'd squeal!" Tim nudged Charlie's arm. "So, you'll come?" Tim's eyebrows rose high; his grin stretched from ear to ear.

Charlie shrugged his shoulders. "Dunno. I'll ask Momma if we can do a work-around. See if I can get away. If the big chores get done first, it might work out."

Two days passed as both moms fretted about the camp-out. The boys argued that they were old enough to camp overnight by the river.

On the third day, Tim carried the clothes basket for Mom into her bedroom and dumped its contents onto the bed.

"We'll be back the next day! It'll be fun. A chance to cool off. Dad taught me what to do in the woods, and Charlie will be there. Promise, hope to di— Uh, I mean, promise to God we won't go into the river.

Please, Mom? I'll catch up on my chores when I get back, like I *always* do."

Mom stood, frowning at the laundry pile. I'll call Uncle Sal. Ask if he could motor down the river with his boat to check on you before you bed down for the night. Just in case."

Tim's ears burned. "Mom! It's only *one* night! We *don't* need Uncle Sal. What can go wrong? I'll be thirteen soon and Charlie is fifteen going on sixteen!"

"Oh. He's that old? And *you'll* be thirteen soon. My, my. I remember the day you were born. You were such a tiny—"

"Mom!"

She smiled. "I can't help it. You've grown some since we first met!"

"Yeah. Some. I'll grow lots taller. And older. Like Charlie. Like Dad."

She separated the clothes by category—shirts, pants, socks, towels, sheets. "Why the rush to be older?"

"Cause Charlie's smart about lots of stuff. When I get older, I'll know as much as he does. People get older, taller, and smarter, don't they?"

"Not always in that order. People learn from others. Your dad learned from Grandfather Elmer, Charlie learned from his dad. Uncle Sal and me, we'll teach you. When you graduate from high school, you'll be smarter and older."

"And taller."

"Oh yes. Taller. Don't *fret* so. You're fine as you are." She smiled and folded the clean laundry. Each item had a particular way of being perfectly creased and folded. Watching her progress through her bedroom vanity mirror, Tim got distracted. He grimaced at his reflection.

Dad and Uncle Sal were long-waisted and long-legged. Tim was short in both areas. His hair was so...red. Grandfather called him a carrot-top. No great thanks to Great Grandfather Wesley and *his* carrot-top. And those bazillion freckles crowded Tim's face like a swarm of ants crossing from one cheek over the bridge of his nose to the other cheek.

"Tim, did you hear me?" said Mom, her stare directed at his reflection.

"What? No. Sorry."

"I said, if you agree to have Uncle Sal check on you, you can go with Charlie."

"Bu— Yeah. Uh, o-okay, yes, Mom."

Tim followed Mom downstairs, each step a lazy thud; not the loud stomping noise he'd prefer to make his disappointment known.

He didn't *need* a babysitter!

Crestfallen, he knew it was useless to argue.

Mom lifted the receiver. "Okay, let's call Uncle Sal."

Tim grimaced behind her back. *Dang it!*

Chapter 4

THE MAGIC MEADOW

At 5:00 AM, Tim got dressed, went downstairs, and sat in Dad's rocking chair by the kitchen window. Although he was ready to head out, it was too early.

Between looking out the window and watching the clock, very few minutes elapsed since he last checked the time. The morning dragged on. His brain and the clock were on different schedules. Or was the clock just not working right? Climbing onto the table, he reached up and removed the clock from the wall.

Mom entered while tying her apron. "You're up early."

"Since five."

"Why are you standing on the table? And what are you doing with the clock? You plan to take it with you?"

"No, I ain't taking it. It's slow. I'm checking it out."

Tim examined the neatly wound wire stuffed into a recessed hole behind the clock. Everything looked okay. The clock's face now showed five minutes had gone by.

Only five!

He flipped the clock back and forth and shook it.

"What are you doing?" asked Mom.

"I think the wire got twisted too tight. It's choking the time, and now it's slow. I'm gonna let the wire hang, like before Dad made that hole in the wall for the clock."

"What? No. Put the wire and the clock back. Don't stand on the table. Get down, please. And after you wipe off the table, please set it for breakfast."

"But Mom, I can fix the clock. It's simple, like water in a hose. That's what Dad said. Electricity flows in a wire just like water flows in a hose. Ever kink a hose? I have, and the water stops. So, I figured it out, just like *that*." Tim snapped his fingers. "Kinked hose? No water. Kinked wire? No electricity." Tim beamed at his clever deduction.

"Tim, it doesn't work that way."

"Dad explained—"

"Well, I think you didn't quite understand what he meant. Clock's working fine. Please put it back and step down."

Tim returned the clock to its framed, recessed wall opening and jumped to the floor, mumbling, "It sure is taking its sweet time."

Mom smiled. The butter in the frying pan sizzled while she beat eggs in a bowl. "Perhaps Uncle Sal can tell you about electricity and how it works." Making her way to the table from the refrigerator, she patted Tim's head. With a frown, he took a quick step aside, pulling away from her hand.

"Maybe," said Tim with a frown. He didn't want to think about Uncle Sal this morning.

"Have you decided which path you'll take to the river?"

"We'll go through the Magic Meadow, the Old Wood, the upper ridge and the Lower Wood. Then we'll reach the Saco. Dad's usual path."

"Sounds like a good plan. Please get the salt and pepper. Drop bread into the toaster and get the butter dish from the fridge. Don't forget the milk. Eggs are ready."

The clock ticked 8:00 AM. A faded red truck pulled into the driveway. "They're here!" said Tim.

"I'm packing the lunch-box. Tell them to come in," said Mom.

Tim pushed the screen door open and hopped down the porch stairs, letting the door bounce against the jamb with a clatter.

"Hello Charlie. Hello Mrs. Wallace. Mom's packing Dad's old lunch-box. She said to go on in."

"Let me guess, peanut butter and apple jelly sandwiches," said Charlie.

"Yup! And Hydrox cookies," said Tim.

"Momma brought strawberry Kool-Aid, apples, and oatmeal cookies she baked last night."

Tim smiled. "Thanks, Mrs. Wallace."

"You're very welcome." Lila walked past Tim to the porch, carrying a large brown paper grocery bag, with her right palm aimed at his head.

Tim scowled with a quick head-tilt, avoiding contact.

Lila paused, smiled at Tim, placed her hand on the back of the bag, and entered the house.

Tim glared at the screen door closing behind Lila. *Head-pats! Grown-ups do that to* babies. *That and cheek pinches. And noisy face kisses.*

He shook his head. Why didn't grown-ups understand? He'd be a teenager in three days. He'd be someone else. Older and smarter. Taller would come soon. He *wasn't* a little kid *anymore!*

Another thing bugged Tim. Whenever Uncle Sal visited, he and Mom whispered. And whenever Tim walked in, they abruptly talked about the weather, gardening, school, or whatever. Why did they do that? He could handle stuff. Were they talking about Dad? That! That's what he wanted to talk about. Why the secrecy?

Helping Charlie unpack blankets from the truck, Tim grimaced. "Kool-Aid. Your favorite, huh?"

"It sure is!" said Charlie with a big smile.

Tim muttered, "Hate the stuff. Milk tastes better."

While Charlie smirked at Tim's grumbling, he carried the blankets to the porch where he folded, rolled, and tugged each blanket tight. He peered over his shoulder. "Momma cut up some old pajamas and sewed them to the blankets like laces so we can roll and tie 'em tight like this. Easier to carry."

"Mom dug out Grandfather's old wooden knapsack," said Tim. He grabbed it from the porch glider. "Tie the blankets on this." He fumbled with the rusty buckles, unable to release them.

"Let me try," said Charlie. After two attempts, he unbuckled the straps and tucked the rolled blankets onto the knapsack's sling.

With lips pressed tight, Tim frowned. First, the clock slowed down; now he waited for Mom and Lila to end that endless chatter in the kitchen while they packed the food. So much commotion for just *one* overnight!

He paced the porch. His simple plan had become as complicated as a family outing to another state. All he needed were sandwiches stuffed in both pockets of his dungarees, and a quick goodbye. They should have been off hours ago! He rolled his eyes in frustration and marched to Dad's old swing hanging on an old maple near the porch.

"Bet you can't swing as high as the porch roof," said Charlie.

"You watch! I'll swing as high as my bedroom window!" Tim pushed himself back to propel the swing with his body, leaning back, stretching his legs, feet pointing ahead to go higher with each swoop. "I'll reach it. Watch me."

"Tim! Help Charlie pack," Mom called from the porch. "And don't swing so hard. That old tree limb could break!"

"I want to reach my bedroom window."

"Please! Stop. Help Charlie."

"Yeah. Okay." Noticing her glare, he corrected himself, "Yes, Mom." His face flushed, the swing slowed, and he planted his feet in the grass, interrupting the swing's movement.

"Need help?" he asked.

With one foot on the bottom step, Charlie examined his bundle. "Nah. All set. You ready?"

"Ready? Me? Been ready since five!" Tim rolled his eyes, shaking his head.

Charlie turned to the door. "Momma! We're going now."

Lila stepped out onto the porch. "Here's the flashlight. Better check the batteries."

"Thanks. I already did. Works fine," said Charlie.

"Goodness! Can you carry that load to the river?"

"Sure can. Tim's got that very heavy lunch-box, so I'll be fine. But honestly, Little Tim's worried he won't have enough Kool-Aid." Charlie smirked at his friend.

"Oh? Here, let me get more." Lila spun around and stepped back into the kitchen.

"No! That's okay. That's okay, Mrs. Wallace. Really," said Tim.

He glared at Charlie. "*Honestly?* Thanks a bunch. And I'm not '*Little* Tim!'"

Lila returned, her hands on her hips. "Is Charlie teasing you? Tim is a nice little boy, so you leave him be!" she said, shaking her finger at Charlie.

Tim winced. "I ain't '*little*' anymore, Mrs. Wallace,"

"Oh. I didn't— My, you are growing. Like *my* little Charlie." She smiled. "Besides, I just remembered you preferred milk. I understand. *My* Charlie is a rascal, isn't he?" She stepped from the porch, grabbed her son's cheeks, turned his head side to side, and planted a noisy kiss on his forehead.

Tim smiled wide at Charlie's look of disgust, with eyes nearly rolled up into his forehead.

"Little Charlie?" said Tim with a smirk. *Revenge! Thanks Momma.*

Charlie shrugged his shoulders and picked up the knapsack. "Ah, she always calls me that. Help me balance this thing while I buckle it across my chest."

The weight of the knapsack pulled Charlie's shoulders back. Standing straight with arms down tight against his sides, he clicked his heels together. "Got everything? Let's go."

Tim made a quick salute. "Yes sir! Let's go!"

Charlie anchored his thumbs around the shoulder straps with both forefingers pointed at Tim. "You heard your momma. I'm in charge for the next twenty-four hours."

"Yeah. That's the plan. Bye, Mom. You know where to find us."

Mom smiled. "Yes. Remember, Uncle Sal lives—"

"Ah, dang it, Mom! Why do you want Uncle Sal to come over and spoil everything?"

"Tim!" Mom rushed down the stairs with fire in her eyes.

Not only did Tim interrupt, but he was disrespectful and complained about Uncle Sal. He immediately wanted to take it back. But it was too late. He had never whined in her presence before. Even worse, he'd done it in front of Charlie and Mrs. Wallace. A red flush crept up his neck and ears. Tim quickly crouched to tighten his shoelaces. He wanted to disappear, escape this fuss he created.

Mom grabbed his shoulders and solidly pulled him up to face her. With firmness in her voice, she said, "Tim, Uncle Sal loves you. That's why he gives you interesting books to read. His farm is up the path along the edge of the river from where you'll be. Tonight, Uncle Sal will check on you. Go to his house if you get scared or need help. He'll bring you home. That is our plan, isn't it? And I don't want to hear you talk like that again."

"Yeah. I mean, yes, Mom."

"And?"

"Sorry, Mom." He stared at his shoes. His feet pulsed with pain. The laces were too tight.

"Okay." With a faint smile, she continued, "Have a nice time, boys." She kissed Tim's carrot top head. Before he could pull away, she parted his hair, fixing it her way. Tim's face grew warmer, but he said nothing.

Noticing his friend's wide grin, he said, "Cut it out, Charlie!"

"What?" Charlie smiled, turned, and walked across the driveway while humming a tune.

Hastily loosening his shoelaces to regain circulation in both feet, Tim picked up the lunchbox, said a quick goodbye to Mom and Lila, and ran up to Charlie. "Sheesh! I thought we'd never get going." With his free hand, he slicked his hair back. His way.

"Why won't she let us camp on our own? Uncle Sal. He's gonna check up on us. Bet that was *his* idea. Humph. I'm old enough. We're old enough. Dang Uncle Sal."

"Why are you angry with your uncle?" said Charlie.

"I'm not angry at him. I'm-I'm just—"

"Angry," said Charlie.

"Mom has a hard time letting go of her 'little boy.' Can't she see I'm *already* grown up? Old enough to take care of myself. I'll be thirteen in three days." Tim stuck three fingers up, shaking them at the sky for emphasis. "I ain't angry. I'm not!"

"You sure fooled me. What's going on in that head of yours?"

Tim avoided Charlie's wide-eyed stare. Like his uncle's stare, except Uncle Sal's eyes appear sunken deep below those thick, bushy eyebrows.

"Ever think of Uncle Sal's eyebrows? They look like his mustache. Yeah. Like his mustache got sneezed up his face!"

"You ever tell him that?" asked Charlie with a chuckle.

"No one I know ever talks to him about his mustache. Or his eyebrows!"

"Why? Will he get angry?"

"Maybe. He's angry at me, anyway. He doesn't like me. I interrupted him once. His big eyebrow got all wrinkly, and he said, 'Be quiet!' without even looking at me. When he's talking with Mom and I come in, he stops, gets up and leaves. Just like that. He doesn't like me. I just know it. I don't want to see him. What will we talk about? Dang it!" said Tim.

With his lips pressed tight, his face flushed pink. He peeked up to Charlie. "Sorry. Guess I got a little angry just then."

"A little? More like a lot to me. That kind of talk don't get you anywhere. It only makes people uncomfortable."

"*You* say that. The other day. Pulling that wrench," said Tim.

"What did I say?"

"'Dang it. Thing won't budge,'" said Tim.

"Not able to loosen a nut in Poppa's truck got me frustrated."

"Why is it different for me?"

"Well, you said it *to* someone because you couldn't get your way. Being rude to people who love you— That ain't good."

"Grown-ups say it. Sometimes. When they're angry. When things don't go right."

"But not at people. That's the worst you can do. And doing it to family makes it terrible."

"There are worse words."

"That's not what we're talking about."

"At least I'm not rude often," said Tim.

"It came out of you more'n once this morning. It don't sound like you. You're just a little kid. Rude kids become mean folk. You ain't one of them. Are you? No. You ain't. So, think about it."

Tim mulled over Charlie's words and said, "I'm not 'just a little kid.' I'll be thirteen in three days.

"Sometimes I just gotta scream out like I just did. Other times I whisper to myself. Sorry it slipped out a minute ago. I won't let it slip out again. I promise."

Charlie smiled and shook his head. "A habit."

"What do you mean?"

"It becomes a habit. You think about it, you whisper it to yourself, and before you know it, it comes out of your mouth. You can't take it back. Soon it pops out whenever you're unhappy about something. It becomes a habit. A bad one.

"When you're angry, you ain't paying attention to anything except being angry. You ain't even thinking about the people you hurt," said Charlie.

Tim clutched the lunchbox handle tighter. He remembered Mom's pained look at his rudeness this morning. With a shrug, he turned and walked ahead.

Charlie followed.

"Do you know we call this place Magic Meadow?" said Tim.

"Yep. Why is that? Any magic happen here?"

"Nope. Grandmother Eleanor named it. It was her favorite place. She used to sit on the porch to watch the deer, birds, butterflies, bees, and dragon flies. She said it was a magical place. So, Magic Meadow. It's Dad's—" Tim shook his head slightly. "I mean, it's our haying field."

"You remember much about your gramma?"

"Sometimes I almost see her."

"In your mind's eye," Charlie said.

"Yeah."

"And your grampa?"

"Grandfather Elmer. Grandmother told lots of stories about him. I remember he was tall. Kinda quiet. His hair and mustache were thick and white. He grew up on a farm, like me. When I was three or four, he'd lift me up in the air, spin me round and round, or bounce me on his knee, and sing 'Old McDonald Had a Farm.' He always wore a straw-brimmed hat. When I'm in our hayloft, I remember that straw hat; how it smelled.

"He died when I was six. Two years later, Grandmother died. Dad said she missed Grandfather so much that she died of a broken heart. Did you know people died from broken hearts? I think about that. A lot. You ever think about that?"

"Nope, never," said Charlie.

"I think Mom's gonna die of a broken heart. After Dad died, she said she kinda died inside. Do you think she'll die like Grandmother did?"

"I think that was a figure of speech on her part."

"Think so? Then what does she mean if she's not dying? Grandmother died. At first, she kinda died on the inside. And when it got real bad, she died all over." Tim's stomach churned. His gut had a knack of reminding him to not focus on troubling thoughts.

"Hey! Let's hurry up. It's hot. We have to get to the campsite, to cool off," said Tim.

With Charlie at his heels, they marched on to the upper ridge. Tim didn't want to think about family members who died. He preferred memories of how they lived. But tears threatened when thoughts of loved ones who weren't around anymore popped into his head. Only his mind could see them. Though it was good to have those memories, they also made him sad.

He would die someday. Would he die of a broken heart? What's the purpose of living if you have to die? Just like a book. Flip the page and you see "The End." Somewhere down a road, there is always an end. Dad was now down a road—at the end.

The word "mortal" popped in Tim's head. The minister mentioned, "mortals die" at Dad's funeral. Tim shivered. Dad died, and Tim would be next. Well...someday.

It ain't fair. Dad should'a lived to be an old man; become a grandfather. Grandfather Wesley Saunders, bouncing my kids on his knee!

"Dang it!" mumbled Tim.

He had promised not to be rude again. But with no one around to hear, who could stop him?

His eyes squinted to the upper ridge beyond the Old Wood.

High up, a cumulonimbus cloud drifted over the distant horizon, heading toward the mountains.

Chapter 5

THE OLD WOOD

Tim's shoes squeaked when water from the occasional marshy area seeped in. Inside his shoes, his feet slipped and twisted at each step, while his friend scaled the uneven terrain with quick, easy strides.

"Charlie, how come you never get your shoes wet? Betcha my toes shrivel like chicken feet."

Charlie smirked. "Step higher and wider, little one."

"I ain't little. I'm just short, and that's temporary. Someday I'll be taller'n you, smarty pants. So stop calling me 'little.'"

"Oh, temporary, is it?" Charlie turned, facing Tim.

"Yep. Dad was tall. So's Uncle Sal. I come from tall men. I'll grow taller when I turn thirteen. You wait and see. I'll beat you."

"That's in three days, ain't it? Better get on it quick. Wait! Wait. I hear something."

"What is it?"

"Quiet. Can you hear?"

"No. What is it?"

"There it is! Oh. It's you, popping and creaking. You must be growing an inch a minute." Charlie poked Tim's arm and laughed.

"Cut it out. Yeah, I'm growing some. But it don't make noise."

"Well, you better step on it," said Charlie.

"I *will* grow taller—soon."

"If you want girls to like you, you gotta be lots taller. When you go to River Fork High, girls won't notice you if you look like a little grammar school boy."

"I ain't little! Technically, I'll be a freshman. And for your information, I don't care about girls?"

"A Freshman? Bet you'll notice girls when school starts. Might even start thinking about them before then. But if you don't grow soon, and you don't beat the girls at getting taller, they'll think of you as that little guy with red hair from grammar school. Besides, girls like to look up to their man."

"They want me to be a giant?" asked Tim.

"Ever notice? Most wives are shorter than their husbands," said Charlie.

"No. I don't care about having a girl look up to me."

"Oh, you'll get there. Like my friend, Little Jason. He shot up like a beanstalk. Now we call him 'Fo Fum.'"

"Why do you call him that?"

Charlie giggled. "Fee, Fi, Fo, Fum! From Jack *and the Beanstalk.* Ever read it?"

Tim laughed. "Does he get angry when you call him that?"

"Do you get angry when I call you 'Tomata Head?'"

"No. It's just a nickname.

"You think I'll grow like Jason did? Like, all-of-a-sudden? That possible?"

"Sure. Instead of hoping to grow an inch, aim at growing two inches! Aim high! The girls will love you. Look at Fo Fum. He's got more girlfriends than you can count." Charlie jumped over the bulging root of an old spruce tree.

"Jason has a bunch of girlfriends. So what? I ain't interested in girls." Tim paused and asked, "Are you?"

Charlie smiled. "Oh, yeah. I have a couple."

"You do? Sounds like Jason's doing better'n you. Anyone I know?"

"Don't think so. They live south of here."

"Where?"

"Georgia."

"That ain't south of here. That's *way* down south."

"Yup. Got family there. We visit once in a while. Met both girls at church."

"At the same time?"

"No, dodo."

"How do you know they're your girlfriends?"

"Letters."

Tim laughed. "What do you write about? You ask them to marry you and live happily ever after?" Tim said the "happily ever after" part with a girlish tilt of his head, a high-pitched voice, and eyelids fluttering.

"Nope. Just wrote about stuff I was doing and told them I liked them. That we'd visit again soon when Poppa traveled south. We'd go to the church picnic. That's a giant family and friends picnic for church members. Everybody brings a bunch of food and lots of sweet tea to share."

"Sweet tea? Why not Kool-Aid, like you give me?"

Charlie nudged the back of Tim's head with his palm. "You ain't my girlfriend."

"Well, I don't want sweet tea. Or any girlfriend either."

"Okay. But you'll change your mind. It'll happen. Yes, sir. It will happen."

"Cut it out," said Tim.

Charlie pointed toward the Saco. "Awright. Let's go. We still got a long way to go to the river." He straightened the straps over his shoulders and stepped forward. Tim followed.

As he walked behind Charlie, the lunchbox got heavier. And heavier. Soon, Tim set the box on a log. Loosening his grip on the handle, he relaxed his fingers and wiggled them. He had clutched the handle too tightly for too long. It had been easier when Dad carried their camping stuff. Tim sucked in a breath and grabbed the lunchbox with his other hand. Now he limped ahead because the box thumped into his leg. "Ouch," he said with a groan. It happened again and again, at every second step. Still determined to carry the box all the way to the Saco, he didn't complain to his friend. He would be strong like Dad. Like Charlie.

As he continued, he silently pledged to act more mature by the time his birthday arrived. Maybe by then he'd be taller, too. He crossed the fingers of his free hand to make sure it happened.

And braver. That's what he wanted to be. His dad's words echoed in his head, "Be brave. Go into the woods like it's your home. If you run from the darkness, you'll never find the light." Tim wasn't sure what the last part meant. But tonight he was camping in the Lower Wood. In the dark. Without Dad.

They walked along a rocky path flanked by a mingling of pine, spruce, hemlock, birch, oak, and maple trees. Honeybees were inspecting the blueberry blossoms scattered on the forest floor.

Charlie crouched, examining the blossoms. "Blueberries will be here real soon! I sure love blueberries!"

Tim hustled and caught up to his friend. "Me, too."

"Now, how can a Tomata Head love blueberries? And how do you get so red? You need a sun tan like I got."

"You ain't got no sun tan." Tim gave Charlie a friendly punch, and they launched into a game of tag, evading each other by jumping over rocks, tree stumps, and bramble bushes.

"I got it, you're a Blackberry Head!" yelled Tim, twisting away from Charlie's reach. A sudden misstep on the uneven, rocky terrain caused Tim to fall, knocking Charlie down with him. Tim rolled and slid on his back while Charlie, unable to roll over because of the bulk of the knapsack, skidded on his side.

As Tim slid under brush, something ripped at his forehead. "Ouch! Ow-w-w!" He stopped his descent by jamming his foot against a sapling.

Charlie grabbed a tree limb to check his fall, crept over to Tim and sat back on his heels. "What's the matter— Jeez, your forehead's bloody! Did you hit your head?" He dug a handkerchief from his pocket and placed it on Tim's forehead. "Looks like a scratch. Momma says head wounds bleed a lot. Here, press on it. That'll make it stop bleeding. Did you hit your head?"

Tim shook his head. "Nah. I'm okay."

Charlie stood and picked up the lunchbox. "I'll carry this for you."

Tim reached out for the box. "No! I'll carry it. Give it!"

Charlie stepped back at Tim's outburst and placed the box on the ground.

With the handkerchief pressed to his forehead, Tim frowned at Charlie. "No one, except me, carries Dad's stuff."

"No problem, Tomata. But you gotta tell people ahead of time. Not jump at them like you just did. People will think you don't trust them. That you think they'll steal from you."

"Sorry, Charlie. I trust you. It's just— I don't know why I said it that way. It didn't come out right. Maybe I'm being selfish. Sorry. You-you can carry it."

"Nah. It's yours. You carry it. No problem here."

A movement behind Charlie caught Tim's attention. "Look. A hawk. He coming at us?"

Charlie turned as a dark bird descended in a slow, smooth glide toward the boys. Then it rose high and circled overhead.

"Looks like it's hunting. Let's get moving," said Charlie.

"Okay, *Blackberry* Head."

Charlie paused and smiled. "Yeah. Blackberry Head. A Tomata and a Berry. Ha! I can write a song about that!" Humming a tune, he walked off composing and singing:

"Walking in the woods one day,

A Tomata and a Berry, hey, hey.

Walking in the woods,

Walking in the woods one day. Hey, hey.

La ba ba ba ba ba lump...."

Tilting his head side to side, his arms marked time in air. The song faded as he walked farther down the path.

Tim tucked Charlie's handkerchief into his pocket and scrambled up to follow Charlie. Although it no longer bled, the scratch burned.

Eventually, the lunchbox seemed heavier than before; he wanted to stop, to sit. Instead, he focused on catching up to and remaining in-step with his friend.

Despite the teasing, the two boys got along like brothers. Few kids their age lived in their neighborhood.

Except there was Roach.

Chapter 6

ROACH

I N 1943, SOON AFTER Roachelle Hallstead was born, she and her mom, Lizbet, moved to River Fork from Georgia for a short while. After Grampa Hallstead died in 1953, they returned once more to help Gram with the farm. Two years later, Lizbet left for Georgia, promising to find a job and a place to live; that she would come back for Roachelle. Therefore, Roachelle stayed behind with her maternal grandmother, Mabel.

Roachelle enrolled at River Fork Elementary School where her teacher introduced her new student by writing "R O C H E L L E" on the blackboard. Roach walked to the board and corrected the spelling by adding the letter "A." Then she said, "I prefer to be called Roach. R O A C H." Her classmates teased her, "Ew-w-w. A roach! Step on it! Step on it." She ignored the taunts, which dwindled within a year. Now fourteen at River Fork High, her classmates never ridicule her name.

This morning, Roach sat at the kitchen table, swinging her leg, barely missing Funnyface, Gram's cat, snoozing under the table.

Gram leaned on her elbows while peeling potatoes at the kitchen's black slate sink. She wore her usual faded blue and green flowered wrap-around apron over an old cotton dress no longer suitable for church. Her one-inch heeled leather shoes revealed wear along with razor cuts to relieve pressure on her bunions and corns, and a broken shoelace knotted together to make it whole.

"Gram's grouchy today. Better watch out, pussycat," said Roach.

"What? Are you talking to me?" Gram turned with her right hand holding a paring knife propped against her hip. Her left hand remained hidden in the sink. "What did you say?"

Roach pretended Gram was hiding the horror of mutilated potatoes in a bloody sink.

"Well?" said Gram.

Eyeing her grandmother, Roach shrugged her shoulders. "Just singing."

"Watch out for the cat. You keep swingin' that leg, you'll kick it in the head." Gram returned to her task.

Roach swung both legs.

The Saunders farmhouse stood visible through the kitchen window. Tim's twelve acre Magic Meadow, Roach's favorite hiding place to spy and hide, lay between the two farms. She once hid in the meadow's tall grass near Gram's garden and watched Gram search for her. After ten minutes, Roach suddenly burst from where she hid; Gram quickly turned and nearly fell. However, she steadied herself by jabbing her garden rake onto the ground. With eyes wide, lips set tight, Gram pointed to the farmhouse. "Bed. Now." Roach went to bed without supper. However, that didn't stop her from hiding from Gram again.

"Meow-w-w!" The cat scrambled from beneath the table, bumped its side against the chair's leg, and fled to the den. Roach had kicked the cat. She dashed after it. "Funnyface! Hey, cat!"

Gram jumped at the cat's cry, and her knife clattered to the floor. With a half-peeled potato in her left hand, she placed both fists on her hips. "Roachelle!" she shouted. "What's wrong with you? I swear. You're such a— Why do you act so *stupid*?"

Roach paused at the doorway, frowning. "I am not stupid."

"I know you ain't. But sometimes you sure act like it! Didn't I tell you to stop? Well? Didn't I?"

Roach turned just as the half-peeled potato slipped from Gram's hand and rolled across the floor.

"Run potato 'fore she gets you!"

"What?" asked Gram.

Roach pressed her lips, squelching a giggle.

Gram's brown eyes darkened as she focused once more on Roach. "Well? What you gotta say for yourself?"

Roach lowered her glance to the old green and beige linoleum. Several scuffed areas barely had any color left. A reminder that generations past had walked in and out of the kitchen and gathered at the table.

"I didn't mean it. The cat was in the way." Her head down, she peeked at Gram. "It wasn't my fault. It just happened," she said with a half concealed smirk.

"So. You think it's funny? Do you? Maybe *you* were in the way. Ever think a that?"

Roach winced at Gram's words, but got distracted by the activity beyond the kitchen window. What were Charlie and Tim carrying across the Magic Meadow? Where were they going? Was it a secret? Frowning, she pushed her lower lip forward into a pout. Her not being invited irked her.

Gram wiped her hands on her apron. "You ain't even listenin'! Well now, you ain't havin' breakfast. Apologize for kickin' Funnyface."

"I didn't mean to, Gram. Sorry, Gram. Sorry!" she replied with her gaze fixed on the boys disappearing over the field toward the Old Wood.

Gram shook her finger at Roach. "Look at me when I talk to you. Go do your chores, young lady. An' don't come back 'til you get 'em done! You hear me?"

With one hand on the counter, balancing herself, Gram stooped over, picked her knife, and the escaped potato. Still frowning, she hunched over the sink and reached for the next potato. With both hands busy, she pushed a lock of gray hair back away from her face with her forearm. But the lock crept back. Jutting her jaw outward, she blew at the lock a few times. It returned. She gave her head a quick snap to the right. The hair floated up a fraction. And returned.

With a smirk, Gram let a grumble escape from her throat. "Gram's grouchy today. Better watch out, Roachelle."

Roach shuffled out of the kitchen. She didn't mean to kick the cat. She even apologized like Gram asked. Now she had to do chores without breakfast! It wasn't right. But she had prepared for times like this.

In her bedroom, she moved her wooden pressed-back chair over to the freestanding armoire—Mom's former clothes closet. From its top, she grabbed the tin box she had earlier discovered in the barn. Now populated with pilfered cookies and biscuits from Gram's pantry, she took two biscuits and returned the tin to its hiding place behind the scroll-work atop the armoire.

With biscuits in hand, Roach went to the bathroom to eat and sip cold water from the faucet. The chipped, streaked mirror screwed to the door offered her reflection, which lured her into her imaginary world.

Mimicking Gram's impatient posture and glare, she acted out her version of the morning's kitchen scene. Stretching her arms with palms up toward her reflection, she whispered, "Potato killer! Oh. My little potatoes. You're falling to pieces. Oh, no. Oh, no-o-o." She muffled her laugh in a towel so Gram wouldn't hear.

After a moment, with a sober expression, she stepped closer, examining her curly hair. Her skin was darker than Gram's and Mom's. Gram said it was like Grampa Hallstead's; neither she nor Grampa blistered from a sunburn.

Mom said I have hazel eyes. Sometimes they're brown, sometimes they're green. Mom called them Chinese Copper. I like that. I'm pretty. Mom said so. Mom's pretty too.

Roach pulled her hair back and twisted it into a bun at the top of her head, away from her neck. It made her look older. Maybe with some pink lipstick she'd look more attractive.

She tossed her head to one side, allowing her hair to tumble down and swing back behind her shoulder. Examining her outfit, all she saw was farm girl wearing farm girl hand-me-downs. She actually didn't mind wearing clothes Gram got at the church bazaar because Gram let her choose. Gram's tastes were old. No. Gram's tastes were *ancient*!

The mirror may have reflected a typical farm girl, but Mom's red crystal necklace, which Roach wore every day, distinguished her from the other River Fork farm girls.

After a pause, she left the room with a grand gesture of arms swinging, the remains of the second biscuit in hand. Once out on the porch, she turned to face the Old Wood.

Why didn't Tim and Charlie invite me?

In sixth grade, Roach noticed Charlie in the schoolyard. Each recess, she watched him play catch with the other boys. He wasn't cute. He was handsome. But he never noticed her, even when she "just happened" to walk by him and his friends. Later, she learned he was one of Gram's neighbors!

The urge to follow Charlie and Tim stirred within her. Dashing to the farmyard, she cried out, "Chick, chick, chi-i-ick!" With the remaining biscuit held between her teeth, she grabbed the feed bag and scattered handfuls at the hens. She rushed as she poured a bucket of water into their large bowl, which led to an eruption of harsh cackles from the annoyed flock. Some birds flew upward; others ran back, avoiding the sudden back-wash of water splattering from the bowl onto the ground. One inch of water remained at the bottom. Two hens pecked away at the shallow water. Others, insulted at being treated with such disregard, squawked at the scanty water sitting in such a large, promising container.

She had named each bird based on its observed personality and habits. Her favorite Rhode Island Reds were Matilda, the attentive and friendly lady who liked to be picked up by Roach, and Oliver the beautiful, dutiful, independent rooster. Esmeralda, the shy old lady of the flock, was next. Not-to-be-trusted Black Heart, an ill mannered Jersey Giant, was last.

Leaving the coop door ajar, Roach bolted toward the path taken by the boys. A few of the greedier hens scurried along after her, while others jumped in brief intervals of low-level flight. Each expected a morsel of the half eaten biscuit which she slipped into her pocket.

Chapter 7

THE LEAN-TO

ON THE BANK, A three-sided lean-to, constructed of saplings secured with twine and big enough for two adults, stood several
feet from the river.

Tim's lower lip trembled. A tear trickled onto the lunchbox
clutched to his chest. "I helped Dad tie those saplings last year."

Charlie nudged Tim's shoulder. "It's okay. I know how you feel.
It's—" His throat tightened. Shaking his head, he struggled to swallow, to speak. After a quick breath, he recovered. "Go ahead, cry. You'll
feel better. It's okay. I know where you're at."

Tim crouched. Tears welled, ready to fall. He shook his head. Placing the lunchbox down, he sat next to Charlie.

"You okay?" said Charlie.

"Miss Dad a whole lot. We shouldn't 'a come. It was a bad idea.
Let's go back home," said Tim, wiping his eyes with his palms.

Charlie wiped a tear from his own cheek. Tim had never seen
Charlie cry. Ever. That's what little kids did. But he remembered when
he was seven, he found Dad sitting at his truck's steering wheel, crying.
Tears streaked Dad's cheeks, his lips pressed together, eyes shut tight,

his face red, nearly bursting. Tim never learned why Dad cried that day. His heart had ached for him then and still did now.

"Charlie?" Tim's voice trembled.

"Yeah?"

"You ever seen grown-ups cry?"

"Don't think they cry much, being grown-ups and all. They keep it inside. Under control," said Charlie.

"Mom doesn't *ever* cry. But I saw *Dad* cry once—" Tim's face flushed. *That sounded dumb. Like bragging about winning a prize!*

"Why? Did someone die?" asked Charlie.

"I don't know. I tried to make him stop."

"Did you?"

"Yeah. I acted silly. He laughed a little. But he was really sad. Sometimes— Sometimes I'm sad. Do you know what I mean?"

"Uh-huh, yeah," whispered Charlie. "I felt that way for a long time after Poppa died."

"You did?"

"Yep."

"I want Dad *back!* It ain't fair for me and Mom, with him gone!" said Tim.

With elbows on his knees and chin in his hands, Charlie stared out beyond the lean-to. In a gentle tone, he said, "You miss your poppa like I miss mine." He wiped his eyes with his shirt collar and wiped his nose with the back of his hand. Tim pulled the bloody handkerchief from his pocket, offering it back.

"Thanks," said Charlie, taking the handkerchief and blowing his nose.

Tim smiled, wiping his cheek with his hand. "That's okay. I wasn't sure where you'd wipe that hand of yours." Tim gave Charley lop-sided smile.

With the handkerchief over his nose, Charlie snorted and chuckled.

The hawk they'd seen earlier reappeared, descended, and perched atop the lean-to. It tilted its head, staring at Tim.

Charlie grabbed Tim's shoulder. "Don't move."

Tim stared at the hawk. "What do you want?"

The hawk moved its head from side to side, eyeing him.

"You better go! Shoo! Careful, or Blackberry Head will get you!"

The hawk bobbed its head.

"Git. Git!" called Charlie, standing, swooping his arms overhead in an arc.

The hawk whistled, "Twee-eee. Twee-eeeee." It stretched its wings as if to take flight, but lowered them, paused and focused on Tim.

Tim yelled, "What you staring at me for? What do you want?"

The hawk bobbed its head again.

"It's creepy. That pointy beak can rip your eyes out. And those black eyes. Like Uncle Sal's. I hate that bird. Shoo. Scat. Get lost! We better go back."

"Why?"

"Dunno. Why is it looking at me and not you? He's planning to attack me. Let's go home."

Charlie thrust himself forward, arms waving at the hawk. It replied with a loud shriek, flew up, but returned to its roost.

Tim stepped behind Charlie. "I'm scared. What's he want?"

"Could be a 'she.' Like I said, when you get older, girls will like you."

"Cut it out. It's a bird."

"Now you're getting picky."

Tim poked Charlie's back. A warning to stop.

Stuffing his hands into his trouser pockets, Charlie reviewed the situation. "Aw, it's only a hungry hawk. Bet it wants food from that old lunch box." He nudged Tim's shoulder and smirked. "It can't eat us. Worse it can do is peck at that red hair of yours. Maybe brighten up its nest."

Tim poked Charlie's back again. "Cut it out."

"It ain't scared of people. Someone must a fed it," said Charlie.

Tim peeked around Charlie. It didn't come closer. "Dad used to feed birds. He said birds are smart. Maybe it recognized his lunch box."

"That must be it! Give me a piece a sandwich!"

Tim opened the lunch box and handed over a ripped corner of a peanut butter and jelly sandwich. It soared high in the air as far as Charlie could throw. The hawk snatched it mid-air, carrying it off into the Lower Wood bordering the Saco River.

"Wow! said Charlie. I never seen a hawk go for a sandwich. Maybe your poppa made friends with that hawk. He ever tell you 'bout it?"

"He talked about all kinds of animals. The little ones were his favorites. Dad said if you talk to the animals, they'd be your friends. That's how Tiny Bear helped Dad and Uncle Sal out of trouble."

Charlie frowned. "Tiny Bear? What are you talking about?"

"He's the tiniest bear in the world." Tim nodded with a smile.

"The ti-ni-est bear?" Charlie repeated with raised eyebrows and a smirk. "Is it a baby bear? You know Mama Bear watches her babies. I don't think a baby bear helped your poppa. Mama Bear would'a chased your poppa clear outta the woods."

"It's true. Not everybody sees him. But, Dad said, when he was nine, he saw Tiny Bear! They became friends."

"Tiny Bear? How'd it get a name like that? You mean a real bear? If your poppa knew him way back then, that bear would be pretty big by now. Or dead."

"He never changes size. Ain't dead either. He's special. The tiniest bear in the entire world! Grandfather Elmer told Dad about him. If you find Tiny Bear, you can ask for help, but first, you gotta send good wishes to people. If you hear him laugh, you know he'll help you."

"Oh, a la-a-aughing bear. Your grampa made up the entire story. It's what people do to entertain little kids! You sure you feel okay? Remember, you scratched that forehead. Maybe your brain's swelling." Charlie shook his head and chuckled.

"No, Charlie, I'm telling you, it's true! If you hear him laugh, your wishes will come true."

"A laughing bear? How do you know they're laughing? Making wishes? Like being rich, having lots of girlfriends and ice-cream?" Charlie snorted.

"No! Listen. You wish for good things to happen to other people. After that, you can ask for help. Like getting home safe. He helps people in trouble."

Charlie's eyebrows met like two sideways question marks. "Well, that sounds goofy." He reached out and tousled Tim's hair.

Tim jerked away. "Don't do that!

"Dad told me about the bear. He wouldn't lie. Grandfather wouldn't either. Dad *saw* Tiny Bear. *I* want to see him, too. But I have to *find* him first! If *you* don't believe in him, we'll *never* find him!" Tim kicked a tree root. His face and neck grew warm.

Did Charlie think him a crackpot? How could he convince Charlie the bear existed? To do that, he had to find the bear. But how? He'd never seen it. He only had twenty-four hours to find the bear, and he needed Charlie's help.

Charlie walked toward a tall hemlock in front of the rock outcropping, which housed their secret cave. "Well, maybe Tiny Bear is real. Momma says, 'Strange things are true, sometimes.'"

Disappointed at Charlie's attitude toward the bear, Tim clenched his teeth and followed his friend.

The cave's entrance yawned wide in the massive rock set on the riverbank. Only Tim, Charlie, and Dad knew about the cave. A natural camouflage of marshland filled with wildflowers, tall grass, cattails, thorny blackberry brush, and vines surrounded and covered the rock's surface. The large hemlock at the entry stretched its branches into a gigantic canopy, further hiding the entryway.

Pausing at the cave's opening for a few seconds, Charlie said, "Better set up camp early so we don't have to set it up in the dark."

Back at the lean-to, they draped the blankets over the framework and anchored them with rocks. Charlie fastened the blanket lace ties to the saplings, then pulled the last tie at the corner of the blanket, tying it back to create an entrance. At bedtime, he'd let that flap down to prevent mosquitoes from entering.

Charlie noticed little bears adorned the laces his momma had sewn together. "Tiny Bear is here! He ain't so hard to find. Stick around Tiny Bear!" He shook his head and chuckled.

Tim watched the lace-bears sway in the breeze. *Hello, little bears. It's true what Dad said, ain't it? I'll see Tiny Bear, won't I?*

Charlie inspected their handiwork. The structure was secure, not likely to collapse, so he placed the flashlight on his blanket. Tim spread his blanket inside and placed the lunch box in his corner.

"Let's get to the cave!" shouted Charlie. As he dashed out of the lean-to, his left foot stepped on a lace end. His right foot caught beneath that same lace, tripping him. He fell face down into the thick grass. "Ouch!" The sudden impact to his nose produced unexpected tears.

"You okay? You hurt? Charlie?"

Charlie paused. "I tripped on them laces." With one hand cupped over his nose, he stood up. His brow scrunched in a frown, his eyes blinked and squeezed shut. His intense, teary grimace revealed his perfect teeth.

"Ahh-h, it hurts. Darn! I better not make fun a them laces again." He dabbed at his nose with the back of his hand.

"Guess not. You got a bloody nose! And watch your language. It could become a habit," said Tim.

"Bloody?" Charlie dabbed his nose with his other hand. As if in shock, he cried out, "I'm bleeding! Is-is my nose crooked? Feels crooked."

"Looks the same to me. Wasn't it crooked before?" said Tim. After a pause, he added, "Just kidding. Looks okay from here. It's bloody, is all. You almost knocked the lean-to on top of *me*."

Charlie walked to the river's edge, knelt on a rock, and dipped his hand into the river.

"Don't fall in!" yelled Tim.

Charlie waved behind his back. His other hand scooped water to rinse the blood from his face. After a few minutes, he stood up, wiped his face with his shirt, pointed and walked toward the cave. Tim grabbed the flashlight and jiggled the lean-to. Satisfied it was sturdy enough, he stepped out, followed Charlie, and handed him the flashlight.

The cave's coolness provided a sweet relief from the heat. The image of a giant refrigerator popped into Tim's head. The farther they traveled down the cave's sloped floor, the cooler and darker it got.

With the flashlight on, Tim's gaze darted from one rocky projection and shadowy crevice to another. Although it was scarier than his bedroom at night, his best friend's presence made him feel safe.

"Caves can be home to bears, bats, and other critters. In winter, bears need a place to hibernate. Hey. Maybe your bear lives here," said Charlie, aiming the light up, down, right, and left.

Beyond the occasional salamander or beetle scuttling across the floor, all they saw were boulders, decomposing matter, shriveled leaves, and damp soil. An earthy smell came from the cave's belly.

Tim kicked a rock, and it jumped up to about Tim's eye level and away. "A-ah! Charlie! See that?"

"What was it? I don't see anything. Where?"

Tim pointed ahead with his feet dancing up and down.

"Stop that jumping!" said Charlie.

"Sorry. Can't help it. Don't want it crawling up my pant leg."

"You scaring yourself. Stop that silly jumping!"

"Okay. Okay. I stopped." Tim turned his head and peered at the cave's entrance. Although he wanted out, he decided against it. He grabbed Charlie's shoulder and pointed. "Aim the light there. See?" His voice squeaked. And cracked.

Why did my voice do that? I sound like a girl. A sissy.

His voice squeaked and cracked a few weeks earlier. Not realizing he had done so, Mom turned to him, smiled and said, "Your voice is changing." She leaned over and continued to stare and smile. She smiled! Days later, his voice got weirder. He didn't know why. His voice never sounded like that. Almost like a girl's voice. Was there something wrong with his voice? With him? Did he suddenly have voice cancer? If he did, why did Mom smile? His mom! Smiling! Why wasn't she worried like him? People died from cancer!

Charlie's light revealed a very large frog standing on hind-legs. Its front legs stretched up the cave's wall. Tim imagined it could reach the top part of the wall in one easy leap.

"Wow! That's the darnedest, biggest frog I ever seen! Bet you scared the daylights outta him," said Charlie.

"Outta me!" corrected Tim.

The frog turned, crouched, jumped, and melted into the darkness.

"Bullfrog?" asked Tim.

"Must be," said Charlie.

"He's so-o big, it's creepy. Betcha he's watching us. What if it attacks? Does New Hampshire have poison bullfrogs?" asked Tim.

"Don't be silly. Relax." Charlie aimed the flashlight and marched on with Tim a half step behind.

They soon discovered a nest filled with baby mice. Charlie examined it. "This one's eyes are closed," he said, pointing to one that had strayed from the nest.

"Looks like he wants to go somewhere. Why don't he open his eyes? That kinda dangerous? He won't see where he's going," said Tim.

"Can't see 'cause he's a baby. Pink skin, no fur. Born maybe today or yesterday. Probably searching for his momma's milk."

"How do we know it's a 'he'? Maybe it's a girl."

"So you *are* thinking 'bout girls."

"Charlie! I ain't interested in no girls! I want to know 'bout the mouse." After a pause, Tim's voice squeaked, "Well? Is it a girl?" He coughed, hoping Charlie wouldn't notice the sudden change.

"Has to be a boy," said Charlie.

"How can you tell? You didn't even look."

"No lipstick," said Charlie with a grin.

"That's a dumb answer." Tim's voice cracked.

"Think so? Well, you can't tell when they're this young," said Charlie.

"We should put it back with the others. So it can stop shivering," said Tim.

Charlie searched around with the flashlight. "There. Get me that small stone."

"Why?"

"'Cause I have to move the mouse."

"You afraid to pick it up? I'll put it back for you."

"No. If you touch the baby, the momma will abandon it. Sometimes mommas eat their babies if they smell a human's touch. That wouldn't be fair, would it?"

Tim's eyes bulged. "They do that?"

"Yep. That's what Poppa said."

Tim handed over the stone. Charlie gently maneuvered the mouse to its nest. At first, it fumbled about, but allowed itself to be guided. Once sensing it was near its siblings, it eagerly snuggled with them. All sat in a rumpled pile, shivering.

"There's a mouse in *our* house. It scratches my bedroom's attic door, then runs around in the attic over my bedroom," said Tim.

"We got 'em too. Cats eat 'em. Crazy thing is, they crack the skull open, like a walnut. If you peek inside, you see the brain."

"Do they eat it?"

"Yep. Seems like it's their favorite part."

"Ugh. No more walnuts for me," said Tim with a grimace. "You think there's a dad mouse?"

"Only way to have babies. You need a momma and a poppa."

Tim stared at the babies once more. "Do bullfrogs eat mice?"

"If something alive fits in their mouth, they'll eat it. Don't worry, they're safe. Momma mouse hides her babies. But you better be careful. I heard they found a half-eaten boy not far from here."

Tim's eyes bulged. "When? What happened?"

"They reckon it was a humongous bullfrog." Charlie snorted and chewed, showing off his teeth with a creepy smile.

Tim frowned. "Cut it out! That's not so!"

But Charlie said it, and Tim could not forget it. His thoughts ran wild. He imagined a half-eaten boy in the arms of a giant frog. Again, he resisted the urge to dash out.

Charlie walked deeper into the cave. Tim followed, keeping watch. Just in case.

The cave sloped downward. The dirt floor gave way to granite rock with streaks of quartz, flint and other minerals. "Ledge," announced Charlie. Tim crouched down and touched its colorful, and pocked surface.

"Betcha Abenaki Indians lived here a long time ago. To keep dry, warm and away from storms. Living on the Saco, they could fish and swim. I wouldn't make a very good Indian, 'cause I can't swim," said Charlie.

"They'd freeze in winter," said Tim.

"Oh, they kept warm. Probably built fires at the entrance. The farther in the cave they went, the warmer it got. And they wore furry hides for clothes. They kept warm enough to survive winter. Moccasins have fur inside. Ever wear moccasins?"

"Nope. But I thought Indians lived in tee-pees."

"Yeah, some did. And others lived in wigwams."

"Wigwams?"

"It's kinda like your poppa's lean-to. Covered with bark. More like a building than a tee-pee. Entire families of Abenaki folk lived in them. I mean, everyone: parents, siblings, aunts, uncles, cousins, grandparents. All in one large wigwam. A really big wigwam is called a lodge."

"How do you know all this Abenaki Indian stuff?"

"Poppa and Grampa told stories of what happened to the Native people, like the Abenaki, and to Negroes like Great Great Grandpa. The Abenaki were natives, but most of them died from diseases the immigrants brought with them. Lots of others got killed.

"Killed? How?"

"War. Fighting the immigrants. Ever see the old Indian burial ground in River Fork? It's called Indian Mound. Indian skeletons are buried there. Strange thing is they're all buried sitting down," said Charlie.

"I never seen it. Why are they sitting?"

"I don't know. I looked it up at the library; nobody seems to know why."

"So, what happened to your great great grandfather?"

"Sailors from big ships kidnapped Great Great Grampa Wallace's parents from Africa and brought them here to America to be slaves. So, Great Great Grampa was born a slave in Georgia. After the Civil War, slavery got abolished, so he traveled north from Georgia by hitching a ride on a wagon. He was eight years old."

"All by himself? Where were his parents?" asked Tim.

"Yeah, by himself. His parents died of fever. Lots of people died of fever after the Civil War. Great Great Grampa, his brother, and three sisters were gonna be sent away. But he ran away the night before they left. He never saw them again. When he got older, he pledged to visit Georgia once a year, hoping to find his brother and sisters. That's how he met his wife, Great Great Gramma Wallace.

"We used to drive to Georgia once a year when Grampa and Poppa were alive."

"Your great great grampa never found his family again?"

"No."

"Where did *he* end up living?"

"He was lucky the driver of the wagon offered him a job and a place to live at his farmhouse—the one I live in now."

"A job. For an eight year old?" said Tim, his eyes open wide in surprise.

"He worked on a plantation at five years old during the Civil War. He knew hard work," said Charlie.

"That wagon driver owned your farm? But you live at that farm now," said Tim.

"Yep. Dr. Remick. His boy, Isaiah, was very sick. So the Doctor took on an eight year old African boy, gave him a wage and a place to live for his help with Isaiah and the farm. When the doctor died, Great Great Grampa, with his wife and his own son, continued to take care of Isaiah and the farm. Dr. Remick's Last Will said Great Great Grampa would inherit the farm after Isaiah died."

"Must have been hard caring for the farm and a sick boy," said Tim.

"It was hard for most people back then."

"I guess we have it pretty easy, compared to them."

"You got that right, Tomata."

Drip echoes could be heard from the farthest end of the cave. "We've never explored the very end of the cave, let's check it out this time, could be your bear is there," said Charlie.

Walking through the granite cave, nothing changed much, except they found a pool at the end, where water dripped from the ceiling.

The dripping sound grew louder, and the earthy smell grew stronger. And, to Tim's disappointment, no bear roamed the area.

From behind, something hit a hard surface. Then another hit, and another.

Charlie turned. "Rocks? Falling? We gotta get out now! C'mon! Stay close behind me." They hurried back, as Charlie swept the light from ceiling to floor, on the lookout for rock ready to fall as they passed through.

The boys arrived at a scattering of large and small rocks on the pathway.

Tim stopped to examine the wall and ceiling. "Up there. That a hole?" He pointed. "These rocks fell, and left a hole in the wall." He climbed a rock-pile for a better view. "Holy cow! That hole's almost as high as my bedroom window! Could be now there's another opening to the cave! And we heard it happen!"

"That looks like a shelf, not an opening. And yeah, them rocks used to be part of the wall," said Charlie.

"Gosh. Better not tell anyone," said Tim in a whisper with a squeak. And a cough.

After a pause, Charlie thought aloud, "More rocks could fall from there." He grabbed one and tossed it up and down in his hand. He aimed the light at the space again.

"If you tell Mom, she'll tell Uncle Sal. Then, we won't be able to come back without a grown-up. Hey, you wanna climb up for a peek?" said Tim.

"Now?" Charlie tossed the rock into the pile and scratched his head. "Maybe tomorrow morning. More rocks could fall. Might be safer in the morning. It's late. Let's explore outside, then get some food. We have a bear to find, remember?"

"I hoped the cave would have a clue for the bear," said Tim. "So far, we found a huge bullfrog and a family of mice. And a scary hawk outside. Hey, you think that hawk will come back?" asked Tim. Charlie didn't answer. He left, making his way back to the entrance.

Tim shivered. "I sure hope it don't come back."

Chapter 8

ON THE SACO

BACK IN THE AFTERNOON sun the boys searched for tiny animal nests. They explored the Lower Wood, the riverbank, the marsh, under rocks, and in thickets. Tim spotted a downed, rotting birch tree, hollowed at its base.

Debris lay scattered at the opening where the trunk lay torn from its stump. Was that evidence of animal tracks? Had something traveled in and out of the birch tree's carcass? Tim peered inside the dark hollow end with the flashlight, and two beady eyes glared back at him.

"Charlie! I found something!"

Charlie hurried over to see. Kneeling at the base, he pointed the flashlight at the critter inside.

"Uh-oh. It's coming out. Better back away, just in case."

"If it's Tiny Bear, you don't need to be afraid," said Tim.

"Oh, I don't know. If that's the bear, he don't look friendly. Could be he's grouchy when someone wakes him from a sound sleep."

The boys backed away from the log and waited. They heard a shuffle and squeaky whines.

"Think he's upset with us?" asked Tim.

Charlie shrugged his shoulders. "I see his nose, and *that* ain't no *bear* nose."

"That's a porcupine!" said Tim as he pushed Charlie away from the log. "Get away from him. He'll shoot his quills at you."

"Who said they shoot quills?"

"J. J., a kid in my class."

"Well. He don't know about porcupines. Just steer clear of them, they'll leave you alone. If they feel threatened, they whack you with the tail."

The porcupine ignored the boys. It ambled from the birch hollow and slowly climbed up the next tree.

"J. J. said porcupines run faster than a panther and when they get tired, they shoot their quills and never miss a target."

"Sounds like your friend makes things up. Ever think of looking these things up yourself in the library's encyclopedia?"

"That's the last time I ask J. J. Jones about anything. All he does is give me nightmares," said Tim.

Laughing till his eyes watered, Charlie wiped his tears as he watched the porcupine climb the tree. "Molasses moves uphill faster than that porcupine can walk." He laughed some more. When he stopped, he said, "Sounds like you have a good plan. Don't ask Genius Jones for advice. I think he makes it up to scare you." Charlie walked away still chuckling.

Tim shook his head, chuckled, and followed Charlie.

How could he ever find the bear? The forest seemed gigantic, and Tiny Bear was supposed to be tiny. How tiny? Very tiny? He hoped the bear was big enough to be seen, so it wouldn't be stepped on. Did Tim give himself an impossible task? He hoped not and crossed his fingers for luck.

Back at the river's edge, Tim said, "I've never seen the Saco this high. You?"

Charlie shook his head. "The river's higher than a half hour ago. Look here, some of the bank collapsed into the river."

Water swirled in pools, wrapping itself around anything in its wake, carving out small chunks of soil from its bank. At least they were *small* chunks. Not a whole lot to fret about.

"Look. A loon! See it go under? Did you know they can stay under water for a long time? How can they do that?" said Tim.

The loon bobbed up to catch its breath where least expected. Each time the loon dove, the boys guessed where it would resurface. After a fourth try, they lost interest.

"I'm hungry. Are you?" said Tim.

"I sure am. Let's get a sandwich and some Kool-Aid!"

With a faint grimace, Tim mumbled, "Yeah, Kool-Aid."

Having skipped lunch, they each devoured two sticky peanut butter and jelly sandwiches. Charlie wiped his sticky fingers on the grass. Tim wiped his on his shirt.

"Your momma won't be happy 'bout that shirt. Better rinse it off later."

Tim gave Charlie a peanut-butter-jelly-mouthful smile. "Yes, Mom."

"Yuck, I'm gonna be sick! Little kids do stuff like that. Thought you wanted to grow up, Tomata."

"Mom wouldn't like it one bit! Can you see the look on her face?" Tim mimicked his mother's angry look with eyes wide and a forefinger pointing at Charlie. "What has come over you, young man?" His voice squeaked and cracked the worst ever. He coughed to disguise his squeak and avoided Charlie's stare.

"Whoa. Your voice *is* changing, ain't it? I used to do that," said Charlie.

Tim's ears and neck warmed. "I-I did that on purpose. To imitate Mom." Tim's voice was normal again.

"Are you sure it ain't puberty knocking at your door?"

"What do you mean?"

"You know. Puberty."

"Puberty who?"

Charlie had taken a big sip of Kool-Aid, which he hadn't swallowed. Tim's response caught him off guard. Unable to resist the urge to laugh out loud, he snorted and coughed, spraying a mouthful of Kool-Aid onto Tim's shirt and face.

Both paused and focused on Tim's shirt.

"Hey! I don't *like* Kool-Aid. And I certainly don't want to *wear* it," said Tim, wiping his face and shirt with both hands. He giggled and burst into laughter, as did Charlie. After a few minutes, the sporadic laughs dwindled to chuckles.

Once quiet, Charlie reached into the lunchbox. "Cookies! Hydrox cookies!" and gave half the lot to Tim.

Ignoring Charlie's warning about eating and acting like a little kid, Tim twisted the cookie wafers apart, scraped the icing with his teeth, savoring the sugary, vanilla-flavored cream landing on his tongue. He swallowed the sweet, creamy icing, then he chewed the two gutted chocolate wafers into a paste. With a wide grin, he bared his paste covered teeth. Chocolate drool dripped onto his shirt.

Charlie smirked and shook his head. "Nah, can't be puberty. *Little* kids eat cookies that way. Your momma's not gonna like that grubby shirt for sure. Never mind rinsing it off! You'd better throw it in the river and scrub it real good before going home."

"I *ain't* a 'little kid.' And I *know* what to do. And what's the deal about that guy, Puberty? Or is it a *girl*?"

Charlie laughed. "Not a guy or a girl. Sex!"

"I don't get it," said Tim.

"Puberty ain't a person," said Charlie. "It's when a boy grows up and gets interested in girls instead of fishing. It just happens. That's puberty."

Tim frowned. "Not for me."

"Oh, you don't have a choice."

"I do so. I won't let it happen. I'll go fishing forever. Just like Dad and all the guys I know."

"It don't mean you can't go fishing. It means you'll get distracted, preferring girls instead of all the things you used to do. You want to grow up and be like your poppa? Don't you? Well, you will. You are. There ain't no choice. Puberty just happens. That's why your voice is cracking. It'll settle down into a more grownup voice. You're becoming an adolescent. And when you get out of high school, you'll become a young adult."

Tim glared at his friend. "Is this the sex talk I'm supposed to get before I grow up?"

"Part of it," said Charlie.

"What else is there?"

"Oh, I think your momma will let you know when it's time. We all go through it."

"All?"

"Yep. Boys and girls."

"Well, why won't you tell me?"

"Ask your momma."

"She don't know that stuff."

Charlie cocked his head, smiled, and poured more Kool-Aid into his cup.

Tim understood that smile. It meant over and out. No more talk about that.

Disappointed at not getting more information about sex stuff, Tim brought his cup of Kool-Aid to his lips. With eyes shut, he sipped the strange sweetened, colored water. With a grimace, he forced himself to swallow.

Did they make this stuff with colored crayons?

Pretending it was plain water, he rinsed his gritty teeth and washed the remnants of cookie paste down his throat. He *could* spit it out, like when he brushed his teeth. But that would be rude. Charlie brought the drink to share. He had to down the stuff no matter how bad it tasted. He shivered and swallowed hard. *How can anyone drink this stuff? On purpose!*

"You think we can climb to that shelf tomorrow?" asked Tim.

Charlie didn't answer. His gaze drifted to the river. "I wonder when Uncle Sal will come. Do you know how deep the river is? Your poppa ever tell you?"

Tim shook his head. "How deep? Don't know. But yeah. Uncle Sal. Maybe he *won't* come!" Tim smiled at the river.

"An Indian baby drowned in the Saco River hundreds of years ago. Now, because of a curse, people are afraid to swim in the Saco. You ever hear that story?" said Tim.

"Yeah. The Saco River Curse."

"I'm not sure what a curse is."

"Momma said a curse is a promise made from bad feelings. It predicts someone will die, get sick, or lose their family, friends, or all of what they have. It could happen right away. Or later. It's like using magic to get even."

Charlie closed his eyes, getting his thoughts together about the history of the Saco River Curse.

"England's King wanted all the land the Indians lived on. The Indians preferred things to be as they had been for thousands of years. But the British took the land, anyway. They chased the Indians out or killed them. So, the British and the Indians became enemies.

"Back then, a Pequawket band of the Abenaki Indian tribe lived on the Saco River right around this area. And one day, a couple of British sailors chased a Pequawket lady while she crossed the Saco in her canoe with her baby.

"They pulled her canoe up to the side of their boat and flipped it to see if Indian babies could swim like everyone said. She tried to rescue her baby, but it drowned."

"That's murder!" said Tim.

"Her husband was a chief. He cried for three days. Then he placed a curse on the entire river—from the New Hampshire mountains all the way to the mouth of the river ending at the ocean in Maine. Every year three white men would drown in the Saco River until every British person returned to England. But the British never left."

"Guess you have to be real mad, huh? I mean, to make that awful curse," said Tim.

"Well, the chief got mighty sad and angry about his baby drowning. And that's all I know. Momma doesn't want me in the river 'cause I can't swim. Guess I'm safer that way," said Charlie.

"But you're not white. Does she know the curse was for white men?"

Charlie shrugged his shoulders. "Maybe she thinks the curse can't tell a white folk from a Negro."

"Dad taught me how to swim when I was little. I can *teach* you."

Eyeing Tim for a few seconds, Charlie smiled. "That'd be fine. But when I panic, the river bottom and my bottom meet pretty quick."

"It's easy to learn. Promise." said Tim.

Before settling in for the night, they set their sock-stuffed shoes at the back of the lean-to. Tim smiled at Lila's lace bears, which appeared to dance whenever Charlie tugged at the laces.

Tim stretched out on his side, patting the soft grass, its sweet aroma filling his nostrils. He felt secure in Dad's lean-to. The saplings supporting the shelter were like long, wooden arms wrapped around him, like Dad's arms.

"Gee, it got dark pretty fast," said Tim.

"Maybe a cloud just blocked the moon. Better get some shut-eye. There'll be lots of chores to catch up on when we get back home, tomorrow."

"And some more time for us to look for Tiny Bear in the morning, before we go," said Tim.

The forest sounds increased in contrast to the quiet inside the lean-to. The mosquitoes buzzed by. A loon's lonely cry faded downriver. Two owls called each other from opposite ends of the campsite. A stiff breeze swelled the lean-to, just a little. The river's current rushed around objects in its path with more force as it made its way downstream.

The river sounds reminded Tim of the Pequawket baby.

Bet he tried to swim. His dad cried for three days. Hm-m. Grown-ups do cry.

Tim's droopy eyelids closed.

A gust of wind shook the lean-to. A branch cracked nearby, accompanied by other sounds from deep in the woods.

He rolled onto his stomach.

Did I just hear a cry? Did someone call for me and Charlie? Out there. A girl? Mom? The Indian lady? Who's out there?

Perhaps he dreamed it.

Go to sleep! Cut out the bogeyman stuff! We're safe here in Dad's lean-to. I'll find Tiny Bear. Right, Dad?

Tim fell asleep.

Chapter 9

THE WOLF

R OACH HID BEHIND TREES, bushes, and boulders, stalking the boys. Where were they going? To the river? To Uncle Sal's farm? Their conversations proved impossible to hear from a distance. Getting closer would betray her mission.

Running and walking soon stirred her appetite. She had missed breakfast. Why hadn't she brought more food from the tin? She found a few scattered leftover patches of tiny wild strawberries to eat. From her pocket, she retrieved the uneaten portion of her biscuit and slowly nibbled at it. If she ran quick enough, she'd be home for lunch. But her curiosity took charge. She wanted to watch. She'd go home soon.

The boys disappeared around a large rock formation near a tall hemlock. Roach dared not step closer for fear they might see her.

She moved to a flat area at the edge of the Lower Wood near the clearing where the lean-to stood. Snapping off a few nearby leafy branches, she created a padding springy to the touch, a comfortable place to sit cross-legged.

After what seemed like forever, the boys reappeared from around the hemlock. They appeared to have fun hunting through the forest and chatting. Later, they sat at the lean-to and ate from a lunchbox.

Roach focused on their food and her own hunger.

I'm hungry. She picked at the threads in her pocket and uncovered one last tiny crumb! Though it wasn't enough to satisfy her hunger, she placed it on her tongue and savored it.

Maybe I should just walk up and say, "Hi." They'd share. But from what they ate so far, they probably don't have much food left. Gram has a meal waiting—I'll go home in a bit.

Gram might be angry, but she wouldn't keep breakfast, lunch, and supper from me. That would be too mean!

Roach brushed ants from her pad and swatted at mosquitoes buzzing her head, legs, and arms. "Darn mosquitoes! I should have worn long pants instead of shorts," she mumbled.

She had enough shade to hide from the boys, but not enough to keep out of the sun's heat. The mugginess made the day seem long and tiring. Sitting still for hours cramped her knees; her right foot had grown numb. She stretched out and rolled onto her belly, propped her elbows on the ground, and placed her chin in her palms. Now she was more comfortable and had a better view.

A soft breeze stroked her face. She closed her eyes, enjoying the cool air. Before long, she fell asleep. Eventually, the world around her fell in shadow. She was unaware that the boys had crawled into the lean-to and had secured the flaps for the night.

Roach dreamed of a dusty country road. At its horizon, a person's silhouette shimmered in the hazy sun. Somewhere, a woman wept. A cool, arthritic hand touched Roach's hair and cheek. A red necklace fell to the ground, and beads scattered onto the grass. A few plunged into the river's murky marsh.

"No!" she yelled, startling herself awake with her hand clutching her mother's necklace securely clasped around her neck.

To her surprise, it was dusk. "It's late! I gotta get back to Gram's!" She got up and stumbled as she ran back into the woods.

Just then, a howl came from deep in the forest. Roach froze.

That don't sound like a coyote. That's a wolf!

But Gram had said wolves were extinct. It couldn't be true, because Roach had heard the same howl twice since moving to Gram's. She spun around, trying to pinpoint its location. Was it headed her way? Perhaps crouched ready to pounce?

A gust of wind whipped her hair across her face, obscuring her vision. She swept her hair back. Peering up, she spotted a massive dark cloud. It moved like someone pulling a gigantic shade overhead, slowly blocking out the moon. The woods grew darker and quieter; the path barely visible.

I gotta go home before that wolf finds me! Gram will be super mad at me when I get there.

"Oh, why do these things happen to me?" moaned Roach.

She ran a short distance and heard the howl once more. A large, dark shape loomed in front of her. She tripped on a root and fell toward the dark shape with arms outstretched to protect herself. But it grabbed her with sharp, vicious jabs and tore at her skin.

"No, no! Ow-w! Stop. Ow-w-w!"

The more she struggled, the more it scratched her arms and legs. However, she soon noticed that if she stopped moving, the tearing stopped too. Her struggle was her own doing. There was no wolf. She had stumbled into a big, thick, prickly bush.

Roachelle sucked in a breath. She had to free herself. Darkness made it impossible to see a way out from the dense bush.

"O-o-oh. Ow! Ow!" Her eyes watered. Had her panicked cries awakened the boys? What if they heard? If they knew what happened, they'd laugh.

But her survival instinct kicked into gear. Let Tim and Charlie find her. She could handle it. This was serious. She knew they *would* help her.

"Charlie! Tim! Help! Help! Ple-e-ease." Her shout erupted from deep inside her chest. At that same moment, the wind intensified, muffling her cry. The moon peeped through the clouds for a moment before darkness swallowed Roach once more. With each move she made, the thorns pricked and ripped at her skin. The cuts burned. Her clothes snagged and tore as she tried to free herself. She wailed as loud as she could: "I want to go home. Gram. I want to go home. Please! Somebody, Help!"

Half crouched, entangled in the brush, Roach heard another low growl from nearby. The wolf again? Behind her? Ahead of her? She listened. Gram said there weren't any wolves anymore. But there it was again. Close by! She dared not move. Another sound got much closer. A strange rumble followed by a...gurgle? Roach laughed and cried at the same time. "That's me! My hungry stomach."

Her relief, though still mixed with fear, erupted into hysterical laughter, making her even more afraid. Afraid of what? She closed her eyes and breathed in and out slowly. She had to calm herself.

Can't have a fit. Gotta get out of here. Bet I'm bleeding like a pig! I don't care if anyone sees me! If they laugh at me, I'll say a bear attacked me. "Ouch!"

With one hand placed on the base of the plant, Roach lowered her head, clenched her teeth, and eased herself up out of the thorny bush, grunting with each move. Scratches didn't matter anymore. With her other hand, she discovered what felt like a thick pine branch overhead. Grabbing the flexible, sticky limb, she pulled herself up through the brush.

Please don't break, please don't. I promise to be good for Gram from now on. Don't break.

The limb didn't break; Roach was free again. She caressed her arms, and with her fingertips, carefully touched her wounds. "It hurts," she said with a groan.

She licked her fingers and tasted the saltiness of her blood mixed with sticky pine sap. A hot bath. That's what she needed. And Gram rubbing salve on her wounds; tucking her in bed. "Gram? I'm scared. I'm sorry. Sorry about the cat."

She carefully stepped through the darkness with eyes opened wide and arms stretched forward, exploring the way to avoid further sur-prises. Sudden distant noises made her jump. With legs trembling, she placed each foot forward. With each step, she prayed she was traveling the right path. Or was it a path?

Roach stopped and turned about, searching in all directions for a clearing or a distant light. Where could she be? Disoriented by the darkness, she didn't know which way to go.

Gram, what direction is home?

A brilliant bolt of lightning lit the distant sky. A rumble followed, ending in a very loud boom. Roach jumped with a squeal.

Before she fell in the thorny bush, she had heard a wolf's howl. Was it on the prowl in this same terrible thunderstorm, too? Could it sniff her out? The thought made her shiver. "Charlie! Tim! Help!" she cried out.

Chapter 10

DISTANT THUNDER

C HARLIE STUCK HIS HEAD outside the lean-to. After a few seconds, he sat back inside. "Did you hear that?"

Not fully awake, Tim yawned, rubbing his eyes with his palms. "I think I heard something. What was it?"

Charlie cocked his head to listen once more. "Think I heard someone cry for help."

"You did? I heard someone calling for help, too. Thought I was dreaming. Maybe someone's out there." Tim scrambled to his knees, peeking into the dark night. "Want to check it out?"

"It's too dark. If we search around in the dark, we'd get lost."

"Call out. If someone's there, they'll answer," said Tim.

Charlie poked himself partially out the entry. Through cupped hands, he yelled, "Hello! Anybody there?" All they heard was the chattering tree branches in the wind.

"Maybe it's the wind," said Tim.

"Could be. Could be a rabbit."

"Rabbit?"

"You ever hear a rabbit when it's caught? Sounds like a woman's scream.

"When I peeked out, the sky lit up. Thunder came up fifteen seconds later. That means lightning hit three miles from here. Boy I sure hate thunderstorms," said Charlie.

"How'd you know it was fifteen seconds? How'd you know it's three miles?"

"After you see lightning, you count the seconds. One-Mississippi, two-Mississippi, three-Mississippi. Then you divide the number of seconds by five. So fifteen seconds divided by five is three."

"Are you sure?" said Tim.

"I know how to divide by five. I ain't dumb."

"No, I don't mean that. I mean, are you sure that's how it's done?"

"Yeah. Grampa taught me. Poppa used to figure how far a storm was."

"Why divide by five?" asked Tim.

"Poppa said light travels faster than sound. When you see lightning you count the seconds. Sound travels one mile in five seconds. So you divide the total seconds by five. Poppa always got home before a storm."

"Why do you hate thunderstorms?"

"They're dangerous! Aren't you scared?"

"I'm not scared," Tim sat up straight. "I used to sit on our porch with Dad to watch thunderstorms."

"Yeah? Well, it ain't safe! Let's get out 'fore it comes." Charlie grabbed Tim's arm.

"Let go!" said Tim, wincing at Charlie's tight grip. "Maybe it won't come."

"No! We gotta get outta here, Tim! Let's get to the cave before it's too late. It'll be safe there."

A boom, a second, and a third exploded in the distance. The wind grew stronger. The blankets flailed; the lean-to creaked. The hair on Tim's neck stood on end, like a cat arching its back, its fur bristling before a fight or flight. Maybe Charlie was right. "Get the flashlight. Let's go!" said Tim.

The boys grabbed and pulled at the bear laces to untie them, but their fumbled efforts knotted them tighter. Finally, in desperation, they stood, pulled and snapped the ties from the frame, and heaved the blankets over the lean-to onto the ground.

They hastily donned their shoes. Charlie, with the flashlight cradled between shoulder and ear, scooped and bunched up the blankets together with the knapsack. With the last blanket tucked under his arm, Tim grabbed the lunchbox and followed his friend to the cave.

At the entrance, Charlie aimed the flashlight inside. It appeared empty, but he hesitated, turned to Tim and announced, "We better go to your uncle's farm. Do you know the way from here?"

"Uncle Sal! He never came, did he? His farm is upriver. We follow the path along the river. But you said it was safer *here*."

"Yeah, well, I'm thinking the cave is super dark. And you don't know what to expect during a storm. We'll leave our stuff inside the cave. It'll be easier to run without it. We'll get it back on our way home tomorrow. Let's go."

They propped their gear inside the cave and hurriedly retraced their steps past the lean-to toward the path with the flashlight in hand.

Annoyed at the water seeping into his shoes again, Tim shouted, "River's higher than when we got here. The path's under water. That's some angry river!"

The wind grew stronger, and the boys aimed for higher ground.

"I smell rain. Coming up soon," said Charlie.

"Yeah! I smell it too."

A brilliant flash lit up the bank of trees ahead of them. A heavy rumble rolled overhead and shook the air, chased by a loud snap. Another flash of lightning followed, with a louder rumble and a terrifying crack. Tim didn't have time to count the seconds. The strike had been close. The wind blew harder, sounding like a constant moan. Tree limbs creaked. Branches fell close by. The boys leaned forward, walking into a stiff wind that felt like a giant hand pushing them back.

"Help us, Tiny Bear," whispered Tim. Keeping an eye on the surrounding trees as he maintained his pace with Charlie.

At six years, he had seen Walt Disney's Snow White chased by the queen's hunter with all that background lightning and wind. He had enjoyed the movie, even if it was about a *girl*. But her panic; that awful witch; and those scary trees had haunted his dreams for a week. Would those awful dreams return?

They traced a path deeper into the Old Wood, avoiding the river as it continued to rise. Tim grabbed Charlie's shirt and shouted over the wind's howl, "Better get back. If we can't stay close to the path, we'll get lost. Let's get back to the cave!"

With an abrupt stop, Charlie turned, aimed the light into Tim's face and said, "Okay! This ain't such a good idea. Maybe your uncle couldn't come 'cause the river's too rough."

Back at the cave's entrance, Charlie stepped forward with the flashlight aimed into its deep recesses. "It looks empty. But keep an eye out."

At about ten feet into the cave, they sat on blankets and watched the storm light the sky in the distance. Within minutes, rain fell hard, hitting the ground like thousands of little feet running toward them.

"Storm reminds me of a dream I keep having," said Tim.

"What's it about?"

"Me and Dad sitting on a fallen tree near the river. It's dark, and the river is high. Rough, like it is now. Dad gets up, says something, points to the river, and disappears into the woods. I chase him, asking what he said. But I'm suddenly in the river, so, I swim to reach him, but I drift away. Trees fall around me. And I get stuck in the marsh's mud. Then I'm in the water again, pulled in the wrong direction. All the while, I'm yelling for Dad.

"Then I wake up in a sweat, yelling, 'Dad! Dad!' in a scratchy whisper. I try harder to yell, but I can only whisper. My brain knows it's a dream. But I keep yelling in a whisper. It's like I'm stuck between a dream and waking up and my brain can't figure it out."

Charlie nudged Tim's shoulder. "That sounds scary. We're safe now. We got here just in time."

"Yeah. You think it will stop soon?" asked Tim.

Charlie didn't answer.

Chapter 11

WHICH DIRECTION TO GO

ONE THING ROACH KNEW—SHE was lost. She didn't know which direction to go from here.

Everyone considered her tough; a tomboy without fear. But a wave of panic washed over her. Running in the dark with the threat of a storm was dangerous. Would she walk off a ledge? Tilting her head to the sky, she yelled, "How can I find my way in the dark? Why did I come here!"

She was curious by nature. Gram often said, "Remember, curiosity killed the cat." Roach always replied, "And satisfaction brought him back." But Gram usually got the last word, with a smirk and a shake of her head, "Well, he been lucky. One day maybe he *won't* get back. You wait 'n see. Wait 'n see."

Was this what Gram meant? Would Roach not get back? Lost forever because she was *too* curious? "No! I'll get back. I will. Just *you* wait and see, Gram."

As if to challenge her, the wind suddenly grew stronger. Lightning flashed in the distance. Thunder boomed soon after. Rain. Rain was definitely coming.

Roach learned about lightning in school; how to be safe in a thunderstorm. Stay inside a house or a car. Don't stand in a field. Make yourself small. Stay away from tall trees.

How could she do any of that? She was out in the woods surrounded by a zillion trees! She crouched to minimize her height, with arms wrapped around her shins and her forehead down on her knees.

Science was her favorite subject. Roach enjoyed spending recess with Mrs. Stark, her teacher, who often said Roach's ideas were "delightful."

"Science makes sense!" said Roach.

"How so?" said Mrs. Stark.

"Animals and people have lots in common. We're all animals. We just look different."

Her teacher smiled, shaking her head. "Science identifies us as Homo Sapiens."

"Homo Sapiens talk, eat, sleep, have babies. Our chickens do all that," said Roach.

"All species have different ways of communicating. Humans can only observe and make conclusions about the other species," said Mrs. Stark.

"I talk to Gram's chickens. I think I understand them. If us Homo Sapiens are so smart, we could learn chicken-talk. Ever wonder how animals notice things before we do? Like when it's gonna storm, they disappear. But us Homo Sapiens get caught in the rain, and in snowstorms."

Mrs. Stark laughed. "Weather prediction by animal observation. Sounds like an excellent project for our next science fair."

Roach licked the scratches on her knees and arms. Her thumb gently stroked the scratch above her eyebrow. When the rain arrived, would it clean her wounds? Help stop the burning pain? Now, her feet hurt from crouching in her tight position. The worst part, though, was a growing cramp in her left calf.

Would Gram be looking for her? Roach hadn't told Gram where she was going. Was anyone trying to find her?

Gotta get up. Get up. Get out of here.

She released her knees and tumbled to the ground. She struggled to stand. The first few steps sent that cramp up her leg, causing her to limp. She rubbed her calf and waddled side to side, wincing with every step until, at last, the pain stopped. She walked forward wary of the dark shapes around her. "You're not scared! *You're* not *scared!*" she whispered to herself.

Another dark shape caught her attention.

That's not a wolf. That's an old tree stump. If there is a wolf, it's probably sleeping in a den, out of the rain.

"Smart wolf, dumb Homo Sapien," said Roach with a chuckled.

If she believed Gram, the chance of bumping into a wolf was zero. But she believed she heard a true wolf howl. More than once since she moved to River Fork. She'd have to talk to Gram because having a wolf nearby was scary.

Wolf or no wolf, she worked on a plan to find her way back.

Listen for running water. If there's running water, it has to be the Saco River. Follow the Saco, and I'll find Charlie and Tim, and they'll *help me.*

With arms stretched ahead, she continued on, listening for the river. But detecting the sound of its moving current among the forest noises and high wind proved impossible.

Her mind wandered back to the time Mom returned to Georgia two years earlier. If she had gone with Mom, she wouldn't be here, lost in a storm, in the New Hampshire woods.

Yeah, like Little Red Riding Hood, trying to find her way to Gram's, with a wolf stalking me? This is scary!

"Mom! Where are you? When will you come back for me? Gram doesn't like me anymore. And I want to go home with you!"

A long, mournful howl emerged from the distance.

"That sure sounds like a wolf to me!"

Chapter 12

LOST

WANDERING IN THE DARK, Roach stepped up a high bank.

"Tim! Charlie! Where are you?" she shouted.

Storm's getting closer! Rain's coming!

She continued uphill. Where did this hill come from? There hadn't been a hill this steep to cross when she'd followed the boys.

I'm definitely lost. Why am I even here?

Home in her room, in bed, wrapped in Gram's warm quilts is what she yearned for; with her head resting on a soft goose down pillow. Two years earlier, she helped Gram make those pillows.

"I can sew pillows too, Gram. Honest, they'll be perfect, just like yours."

"I know you can do what you set your mind to. Just to be sure you do it right, let me show you how I put 'em together."

Gram grabbed a handful of feathers from a burlap bag and stuffed the feathers into a freshly sewn pillowcase. Once filled, she folded and pinned the pillowcase end shut and treadled her old Singer sewing machine to stitch the folded edges together. "You sure you can do this?"

"Honest, I can." Roach plunged her hand into the burlap bag and smiled as she stirred the down feathers into a little whirlwind. A few feathers floated out of the bag.

Gram frowned a little. With a wary eye, she watched the feathers settle to the floor. "Okay. Stuff the pillowcases—slowly. Then fold the edges and pin 'em. Later, I'll teach you how to sew 'em. Be back in a bit. Let me know if you have a problem." Gram got up and hesitated at the door, glanced at Roach, shook her head, and left the room.

Thirty minutes later, she returned, halting in the doorway. With a screech, she bent over, one hand on her knee, the other at her chest.

"Gram? What's wrong? Are you having a heart attack?"

"What? Oh, my! No!" Gram struggled to catch a breath. "Dear child, Ro-o-oach! No. No heart attack. Get Gram a chair or-or I'll fall over!"

Gram laughed! She never, ever laughed that hard. It alarmed Roach. Gram was old. She could fall. What would Roach do if Gram fell to the floor? Roach hurried, slipped the stool behind Gram, and guided her rear end. It landed with a thump.

Roach's confused expression and eyes bulging with concern drew a high-pitched cackle from Gram.

Roach extended her lower jaw, aimed it sideways, and blew up at an annoying feather on her cheek. "What is it, Gram?"

Gram took a deep breath, snorted, burst into giggles and more laughter.

Roach moved closer; her face inches from Gram's, and looking into her grandmother's eyes caused Gram to shriek and laugh so loud that Roach stumbled backward. What was wrong?

Gram reached forward and plucked feathers from Roach's hair. "You-you look like a chicken!" said Gram, between her laughter and cackles. "Look at yourself in the mirror.

Standing at the mirror behind the door, Roach did think of chicken with all those feathers stuck to her. Feathers littered the floor. Some floated about. Gram called out, "Chick chick chi-i-ick!" Roach crowed, "Cockle doodle do-o-o," mimicking Oliver. Both giggled as they scooped feathers from the floor and plucked them from Roach.

Memory of that event, when compared with her present crisis caused Roach to moan out loud. That had been a pleasant time. When did she and Gram stop having fun together? What changed? Now, Gram seemed angry most of the time.

Why isn't Gram nice anymore?

"Charlie! Tim! Where are you? Help me. Help! I want to go home," Roach howled out as loud as she could. Perhaps someone would hear her. Help her. How else would she find her way?

The wind intensified, and rain burst from the darkness. Torrents of large raindrops pounded the ground like tons of rubber balls and drenched her. She ran with difficulty. She slipped sideways and forward. She struggled to stay upright. Stepping into a puddle, she skidded flat onto her back with an oozing splash of pine needles and watery mud.

"Ow! This is horrible! Why, why, why did I come? Why didn't I mind my own business and stay with Gram?"

The slick mud made standing nearly impossible. Eventually, she recovered her balance and slowly plodded forward with purpose despite the downpour and mud.

"Charlie! Tim! Where are you?" she whimpered.

Climbing farther up over the bank, she grabbed at a vine covered rock wall for support. Trees abutted the wall at odd angles. With her hands guiding her, she climbed over and around tree limbs and trunks that lay or stood in her way. Where would this blundering in the dark lead her? Would it be to Charlie?

If Charlie knew I got lost in this storm, he'd come find me and wrap his arms around me. Then I'd be safe. Yeah. If only.

There it was again. A howl mixed in the wind. Was the wolf following her, or warning her of danger? Each time she heard it, something happened to her. Why would a wolf help her?

Roach stepped over a downed tree trunk, plunged into a depression; fell hard on her rump, and continued down a slurry slope of mud. She jostled to her side and rolled onto her stomach, all the while screaming, "No-o!" She grabbed for anything solid poking up from the slurry that might slow her descent, a root, a rock, anything.

The rain fell hard; the slick mud splattered, slapping at her face with a sickening, sweet-smelling ooze that threatened to fill her mouth. Its texture was like a mashed-up soup of earth and rotted leaves that had scattered and compacted over time from the forest floor. She gagged at the gritty, nasty taste. She coughed, spit out the filth, closed her lips tight, and continued to slip farther down the slope. From below, she heard it. Finally! She heard it! The river! She would fall into the river!

"No! No! Not the river.! Not now. No, no!" In a panic, Roach clawed at the mud with her fingers, and hammered the toes of her shoes into the soft ground.

She caught a tangle of exposed roots from an old spruce tree. The roots had, over many years, twisted into a mass that formed a hollow oval, like a bowl or a cradle. Roach clutched a root, stopping her descent. Examining the root with her other hand, and able to see bits of the root with each lightning strike, she crawled into its oval shape. Although uncomfortable, she laughed and cried at this lucky find. She settled into the cradle; slipped her left arm under one root to hold on; her other hand grabbed the smooth bark of another, nearby root.

Though finally anchored in place and secure, she felt miserable.

"Charlie? Tim? Somebody? Anybody! Help me," she cried out.

No one answered. Rain, thunder, and lightning were her only companions.

Alone in the storm, she thought of Gram. And poor Funnyface. She hadn't meant to hurt the cat, just to annoy it. Why did she do things like that? Charlie and Tim. Why hadn't they invited her to join them this morning?

The storm continued to light the sky at intervals. Rain pounded her body. Thunderclaps made her tighten her hold on her tree root. She shivered so hard it seemed the ground shook beneath her. Would the muddy earth suck her down deep into itself? Like quicksand? Did New Hampshire have quicksand?

After a long while, Roach relaxed, just a little. Resting her head on her shoulder, she let go of the second root and covered her face with her hand, protecting it from the pummeling rain.

Each lightning strike seemed brighter and closer than the last, pro-viding her with snapshots of her surroundings as she peeked through her fingers. Each thunderclap grew louder than the former. Between strikes, Roach experienced absolute darkness.

"Rain, please stop," she whispered.

Shivering and exhausted, could she sleep? Sleep would bring tomorrow sooner. She'd go home at sunrise. She wasn't trying to annoy Gram this morning. Not on purpose. Why did Gram get so upset with her?

The storm sounds melted into a rhythm, like a lullaby, as Roach rested in the embrace of the giant spruce tree.

At the edge of sleep, she muttered. "Sorry Gram. Funnyface. Hey cat! Charlie? Just wanted to see, is all."

She clung to her cradle. Drifting in and out of an uncomfortable sleep, she ached as the roots pressed against her ribs and shins.

In a lightning flash snapshot, Roach saw a man. A tall man walking through the shadows. A shadow-man?

Did the shadow-man see me? Why is he here? Is he looking for me?

She blinked, and he was gone.

She closed her eyes, giving in to a deep sleep, melting into the rhythm of the storm. Or was it the rhythm of someone chanting a lullaby? A mournful howl again erupted in the distance. Her body convulsed in a shiver, and her hand tightened its grip around her root. Why hadn't the wolf appeared? She felt its presence. Had it spoken to her, warning her? Warning her of what? That must be it. It warned her to be careful. Each time she heard it, something happened to her. But there were no wolves in New Hampshire, Gram said so.

Chapter 13

THE SHELF

F OR AN INSTANT, LIGHTNING illuminated the cave walls. In the next, blackness filled the cave. This cycle revealed eerie snapshots of Charlie's fearful facial expressions and movements. Tim supposed he too appeared in similar, eerie staggered snapshots.

Huddling closer, Charlie leaned against Tim's shoulder. "You scared?"

Tim nodded. "I thought it would be fun to be in a storm. Now I'm scared."

"Yeah, it ain't safe being out there. This is the darnedest, biggest storm I ever seen," said Charlie.

They sat on rumpled blankets, facing the spectacle. Lightning struck, thunder boomed and crackled without interruption. The heavy rain fell hard onto the ground. A curtain of water and mist obscured the entrance. The wind howled louder. Beyond the lean-to, visible from the cave, lightning illuminated the sky, silhouetting the trees. Limbs shook like fists at the murky heavens, protesting. A nearby tree snapped and crashed. The thunderous roll overhead unmasked nature's fearsome power.

Charlie gasped and drew a blanket over their heads. For a split second, a bright light lit the cave, penetrating the darkness beneath their blanket, and quickly vanished. An immediate deafening snap and a ground-trembling boom echoed around them. A large limb from the hemlock crashed at the entrance, part of it landing inches from where they huddled.

Tossing aside the blanket, Charlie scrambled up, grabbed Tim's arm, and dragged him out of harm's way while aiming the flashlight into the cave's interior behind them.

"Holy moly," Tim yelled, "look at the size of that thing?"

"Grab your stuff! Follow me!" They ran farther into the cave. "This ain't a regular thunderstorm. It might be a-a hurricane. Or tornado. Gotta hide somewhere so it won't get us!" said Charlie.

"I know about tornadoes, but I never seen one. What do we do?" asked Tim.

Aiming the flashlight ahead, they raced down the cave's interior, but Tim's foot slipped and twisted in a crevice. Reaching out to break his fall, his hand struck the sharp edge of a rock, and the lunchbox clattered at his feet. "Ouch!"

"You okay?" said Charlie.

"Yeah, I'm okay."

"There!" Charlie pointed the light to the ledge. "We'll climb up there."

Hours earlier, Tim wanted to explore the shelf. Now he was hesitant. Would something be up there hiding from the storm?

Examining the wall's surface with his palms, Charlie handed the flashlight to Tim. "Shine the light on me!" he said.

Slipping the knapsack over his shoulders, he buckled it, tied the blanket corners end to end, and cinched the last one to his belt. He grabbed at rocks protruding from the wall's rough surface and worked his way up the rock wall with blankets trailing from his waist. The image of his friend climbing with a long train of fabric reminded Tim of the peacocks at Benson's Animal Farm Zoo down in Hudson, New Hampshire.

"Now point the light ahead of me," said Charlie.

The flashlight firm in his grip, Tim lit the way as Charlie explored the wall for fissures and protruding rock to grab and step on in his climb up to the shelf. With the light held high, and his head held in a constant up angle, Tim's arms grew weary, and his neck ached. He worried about Charlie slipping and falling. Could he catch him if he did? And the climb seemed to take forever.

Charlie finally heaved up onto the shelf, knocking rocks and pebbles over the edge. "Watch out!" he yelled. Tim flung both arms atop his head for protection and stepped away. A scattering of rocks landed at his feet.

Charlie whooped in unison with a sudden, ear-splitting thunderclap.

"What's happening? You okay?" Tim yelled in alarm as he backed away and stumbled over the fallen rock behind him. He landed hard on his behind. The flashlight slipped from his grasp, hit the floor, flipped, and rolled away.

"I'm okay. Wanted to scare off whatever might be in here. Where's the light? I need light!"

"I dropped it."

"Pick it up."

"Gotta find it first!" Unable to see, Tim crawled, pawing for the flashlight. There it was farther down the slope, emitting a dim glow. But before he reached it, the light flickered out.

"I-I think it's broken."

Charlie mumbled what sounded like an angry response. Perhaps upset with Tim for dropping the light? Tim closed his eyes and clutched the flashlight to his chest.

"You sure the flashlight doesn't work?" said Charlie.

Tim switched the power button back and forth. Nothing! He shook it. Nothing! He screwed the lens off and on. Nothing happened. "It-it won't work. I'm sorry." Near tears, his voice wavered. "I didn't mean to drop it."

"Hey! Tim. Hey. It's my fault. I yelled, and scared you, is all. We'll figure this out. Okay?"

Tim wiped tears welling in his eyes with his shirtsleeve and nodded.

After two quick breaths, he whispered, "Tiny Bear, please help us!" Fumbling with the flashlight, switching the on-off button, removing the lens, replacing it once more, he gave it a violent shake. "Please!" he yelled at Tiny Bear—wherever he was. It lit up! "Holy cow! It works." He smiled wide, caught his breath, and whispered, "Thanks, Tiny Bear." Happy in the belief the bear answered his plea, he smiled and whispered again. "Thank you."

"Great. Grab the blanket?" said Charlie. He wiggled the blanket hanging from the shelf. On tiptoe, Tim reached up. "It's too high. Even if I grab it, I won't be able to hang on and hold the flashlight, too."

"Put the light in your shirt pocket so you can see up!" Charlie hung his arms over the edge, lowering the blanket a couple of feet. "Can you reach it now?"

"Yeah. But what about Dad's lunchbox?"

"Tie it to them laces."

Tossing the blanket around, Tim found a lace tie and secured the lunchbox. "Done. Now what?"

"Hold on tight. Don't let go, no matter what. I'll pull you up. Ready?"

Tim nudged the flashlight in his pocket, patted the lunchbox, and clutched the blanket with both hands. "Ready."

Charlie pulled. The uneven rock wall scraped and poked Tim on his ascent. Terror struck twice when he heard the blanket rip—his weight preventing the blanket from traveling with ease over rough sections of rock. With teeth clenched, he searched the uneven wall for footholds with which to push himself upward, relieving some of the stress on the blanket.

Charlie gripped Tim's forearm. "Put your elbow over the edge and pull yourself up. I'll help you. Look at the shelf and go for it. See yourself on the shelf. Imagine you're that boy on the shelf. Be that boy on the shelf! You'll make it okay."

Seizing Tim's belt, he pulled him over the edge. Finally up, both scrambled to the back of the shelf. Neither one spoke. Charlie gathered and stashed the knapsack and lunchbox in a far corner. He spread blankets, still tied end to end, for them to sleep on and said, "We'll climb down in the mornin'."

Exhausted, the boys leaned back against the cool wall. Confidant they were safe from the storm, they fist-bumped each other's shoulder for a job well done.

Charlie switched off the flashlight.

Lightning, thunder and rain raged on, and they were safe!

Chapter 14

A MAGICAL PLACE

Each lightning strike snapped with a force greater than Tim had ever experienced. The strikes partially lit the cave; the thunder's rumble continued on and on, and his bravado about thunderstorms melted away.

"Will lightning reach us? Dad said it can travel sideways," said Tim.

Massaging his aching biceps, Charlie yawned. "We're okay here. It's late. I'm tuckered out. Let's get some shut-eye. We'll go home first thing in the morning." He switched on the light and crawled to a hollow space in the rock wall behind a triangular shaped boulder. There, he placed the backpack and secured the lunchbox behind it. Spreading the end blanket over the boulder, he anchored it to the backpack's framework. The combination produced a place to lean against—a well-anchored blanket for a backrest.

Removing and setting their shoes and socks aside, they bundled themselves in the remaining connected blankets, and Charlie switched off the flashlight.

"Will the rain stop soon?" asked Tim.

"Yeah. Storms don't last long. Should be over in an hour, or so. We'll be home in the morning."

"You think it's a tornado?"

"Nah. Not noisy enough."

"Not noisy enough? How noisy is a tornado?"

"Grampa said they sound like a freight train coming at you. Ever hear a freight train?"

"Yeah. So, you think it's a hurricane?"

"Yep. We need some shut-eye. Lots to do in the morning."

"Okay. A hurricane ain't so bad. G'night, Charlie."

"Ain't bad? Ha! G'night, Tomata."

Charlie pulled a blanket up to his chin. Tim snuggled closer to his friend for security. Soon, Charlie's breathing became deep, slow, and steady.

Tim watched the lightning project shapes onto the cave wall for a second or two. To occupy himself, he identified each shadowy shape. It seemed a magical place with floating faces, birds, clouds, and...a tiny bear!

The bear lingered. It swayed its head side to side. It stood up on its hind legs. Was it waving its paw? Tim quickly stuck his hand out, waving back, whispering, "Hello, Tiny Bear. Will you stay with us?" The bear got down, lowered its head between its front paws for a moment, stood up again, and vanished.

Was that the bear?

Probably just a shadow on the wall.

Will we find Tiny Bear? I gotta, 'cause I need— No. We need his help!

Chapter 15

A PLEA

TIM SHOOK HIS HEAD and blinked several times to stay awake. Suddenly, he found himself in a place he'd never been before.

"What is your name, Sir?" asked the bearded frog, its large, gleaming black eyes focused on Tim.

"I'm Tim. Charlie calls me Tomata Head. Who are you?"

"My name? Why, dear Sir, I am Salubrious Frog! Tomata Head? Indeed! You *are* a little red in the cheek, aren't you? And your hair is so *red*. Dear, dear, what do you make of that?"

Tim's hand touched his hair, brushing it back. "Yeah. Mom says it's cute. It's not. It's embarrassing."

"Embarrassing? Look at me. Who ever saw a frog like me? Other frogs find me objectionable. Just plain ugly! Now that is embarrassing. Wouldn't you agree, Sir?"

Examining its giant size, Tim noted the frog's scruffy beard and watery eyes. Its skin was dark brown, mottled with yellow and green, and bumpy. It had thick webbing between the fingers. Or were they toes?

The frog jumped up into the foliage of a tall hemlock and disappeared among the branches. A wind howled, tossing the tree side to side, making it difficult for Tim to stand upright. Crouching at its base, Tim called up, "Mr. Frog! Don't go! Salubrious, Salubrious Frog. Come back! Please!"

"What do you want, Sir?" said the frog with a booming voice from somewhere up high.

"I want to go with you. Take me with you to see the bear."

After a pause, the frog jumped down. Now inches away, face to face, Tim felt the coolness of its skin. It contrasted with its warm, wiry beard. Stray whiskers tickled Tim's nose.

"What did you s-say, S-sir?"

"I said, 'take me with you to see the bear.' Tiny Bear! I-I need to see him."

The frog sat up and stroked his beard. "Tiny Bear, Sir? What do you know about Tiny Bear?" he asked, pointing a bony, webbed finger at Tim.

"Dad said the bear rescued him once—Dad and his brother, Uncle Sal. Tiny Bear lives somewhere in the Lower Wood, right here on the Saco. I just know it. And now I need to find him. Take me to him. Please?"

"And your mother, what about your mother, Sir?" the frog whispered.

"Mom worries a whole lot since Dad died."

"Died? Died, Sir? Your dad left you? Left your mother and you alone?"

"Dad didn't leave. He...died."

"Your father left you and your mother when he died." The frog's eyes glowed orange, leaving a dark slit where a large, black pupil used to be. He squinted. "Why do you seek the bear, Sir?"

Tim didn't answer. He struggled, desperately holding the threat of tears at bay.

"Your eyes tell a story, Sir. Do you want me to tell what it is?"

"They do? What kind of story?"

"You are angry. You are very angry with someone. That is why you wish to speak with Tiny Bear. Am I correct, Sir?"

"No!"

"Oh, my dear Sir. The eyes tell the truth! To see Tiny Bear, you must tell the truth. You must not be dishonest. Tiny Bear cannot listen if you are so."

"He helped me and Charlie with the flashlight today. I know he did. Tonight, he visited me in the cave. I want to see him again. Can you help?"

"Help? Help you, Sir?"

"Yes. Take me to him."

Croaking louder and louder, the frog turned, jumped high into the hemlock once more, and vanished. Although gone, his croak echoed throughout the cave.

Tim awoke with a start to Charlie's croaking snore.

Tim re-positioned himself in his blanket. The cave was still dark. How late could it be? Was it close to morning? The wind still howled outside. Flinching with each distant boom, he closed his eyes to calm himself.

Charlie's rhythmic breathing comforted him. Even though the snoring grew louder, Tim didn't mind. With a chuckle, he assured himself that *he* certainly didn't snore. Mom would have said so.

Soon, Charlie's buzzing snore lulled Tim into a restless half-sleep. If only he could sleep like his friend. Tim counted lightning strikes. "One, two, three, five, nine, eighty-teen, three-teen—" His head bobbed. He slept for a while, but later lay awake. Well, half awake. Why couldn't he fall into a deep sleep like Charlie? A pillow would help. Warm milk would do the trick. But all they had was that awful Kool-Aid.

Tim crawled out from under his blanket, careful not to rouse his friend. He squinted his bleary eyes, focusing. A spec of early morning light reflected from below. The cave opening, barely visible from the shelf, looked smaller. The cave floor just...moved? Or did it? What he saw didn't make sense.

Leaning forward, his foot bumped Charlie, who grumbled, half turned and readjusted his position. Tim crouched at the edge of the shelf, staring below.

Something is moving. Something big. Why is the ground moving?

"Earthquake!" Tim's voice cracked, this time with a very high pitch, which he didn't notice.

Gasping for breath, he half whispered, kicked at his friend's ankle, "Charlie, Charlie!"

Charlie groaned. "What?"

"Look! The cave is moving."

"What are you talking about?" Charlie turned in his cocoon. "You dreaming, Tomata?"

"No! It's an earthquake!"

Charlie scrambled out of his bedding, joining Tim at the edge of the shelf. He looked down to the cave's floor, to the entrance, and up at the craggy rock overhead.

Watching his friend's shadowy profile, Tim waited, his heart pounding. "What are you listening for? What's wrong?"

"We're in trouble. We're in big trouble," said Charlie.

"Why?"

"Can't you hear it?"

"Is it an earthquake?"

"No. An earthquake would make this place fall apart. We wouldn't be able to sit still. Listen. What do you hear?"

"Water. I hear water." Tim looked down. The floor moved, reflecting the light he had noticed before. A gurgling noise and the lap-lap of water accompanied the motion of the swirling light on its surface. "It's water! Just below us!" Tim caught his breath. A chill crept up his spine. He sat up, pushing himself away from the edge for fear of falling. "Why's there water in the cave?"

Charlie switched on the flashlight. "The river. It flooded the cave while we slept," whispered Charlie. "Can't go anywhere now. Have to wait 'til it goes down again. Looks like the water is maybe six or eight feet below us. Hard to tell. The floor slopes downward, so the water's way over our heads."

"That's a lot of water! We have to get outta here! *How* we gonna get out?" said Tim.

Charlie switched off the flashlight. "We'll get out. Just relax, it'll go down before you realize it. This is a river, it travels. Has to go somewhere. It'll go down," said Charlie.

With nothing else to do, they sat at the back of the shelf.

"It's a good thing we found this spot, ain't it?" said Tim.

"A good thing? Yeah, a good thing."

The light outside remained dim. The thunder distant. The wind strong. Perhaps it was very early in the morning. Morning, with a whole lot of water to move downriver. When would they get home again?

Tim blamed himself. He talked Charlie into coming. Now the river trapped them. More important than ever, he had to find Tiny Bear. He just had to. They needed him. *Now!* But where would he look? Why hadn't he asked Dad more questions about Tiny Bear?

Crouched next to Charlie, thinking of workable solutions for escape, Tim eventually grew weary. As he fell asleep, he wished he had his pillow. Bost mostly, he wished they had not come.

"Dad. It ain't fair. Come back," he mumbled in his sleep.

Tim leaned forward, peering up through the leafy fronds of the hemlock. He sensed the frog was still there. "Salubrious Frog! Come down!"

"What do you want from me, Sir?"

"I need your help."

The frog peeked down through the tree's branches at Tim.

"Salubrious Frog, please. We gotta find Tiny Bear."

"How do you know I can help, Sir?"

"I'm not sure. But I know I have to ask you to help me— Us."

"Us? Who is 'us' Sir?"

"My friend Charlie and me. He's the one who calls me Tomata Head. Remember?"

"I remember Sir Charlie. I remember."

"Please don't leave us behind again."

The frog descended headfirst from the giant tree. As he got closer, his eyes glowed, changing from black to yellow to black again. Once he touched the ground next to Tim, he stood upright, as tall as the giant hemlock he'd descended. His front legs stretched upward; his voice boomed. "Why not, Sir?"

Distracted by the frog's ever changing qualities; its sudden gigantic size, Tim covered his ears. His own voice faded to a whisper. "Why what?"

"Why must I not leave you behind, again, Sir?"

Frowning, searching for an answer, Tim shut his eyes. "I'm afraid!"

"Speak louder. I can't hear a word, Sir!"

How could it not hear him? Annoyed with the frog, Tim shouted, "I'm afraid!"

In one swift movement, Salubrious Frog bent down, whispering in Tim's ear. "Why are you afraid, Sir?"

Tim paused. "I don't know. Things happen, and I don't know what to do."

The frog smoothed his beard. "What things, Sir? Things? Things are everywhere. Are you afraid of all things that happen? Are you also afraid of things that have not happened? Things that just are, Sir?"

Stammering, Tim's face flushed. "I mean-I mean, about things that-that already happened! Dad died. I feel bad and don't know what to do. Mom feels bad and I don't know what to do. Now Charlie and me, we're in big trouble. I don't know what to do. Charlie's scared, just like me. Nobody knows where we are. Who will rescue us? What am I supposed to do?"

"Why must you do anything, Sir?"

"I feel like I'm supposed to do something, but I don't know what it is."

"Do you mean, Sir, you must act differently, do something unusual?"

"Maybe both. I'm not sure."

"What would your dad say, Sir?"

"Dad? He used to say, 'If you run from the darkness, you'll never find the light.' I don't know what that means. Do you?"

Scratching and smoothing his beard, Salubrious Frog took a breath. "Yes. I do, Sir."

"Am I supposed to not be afraid of anything? Like Dad? I wish he wouldn't have gone away like that."

"Sir! Ah! But you tell me he didn't go away. He died!" Salubrious Frog stooped down, his eyes grew wider, his voice a mere whisper. "Are you angry with Dad, Sir?"

Tim's face flushed, and his teeth clenched. He fought the threat of tears. "No! I'm not angry with Dad! Dad is dead. He died!"

"Oh, my, Sir! You are angry at someone. Yes, you are! Your eyes are cold. Let the pain come. Let the light in, Sir. Don't be afraid of the dark." At that, Salubrious Frog crouched on his large hind legs, pushed himself high off the ground, hopped into the hemlock's upper branches, and disappeared.

"No! Come back. Don't go! I need to find Tiny Bear!"

"Hey, Tomata Head. Hey, hey. What's wrong?" said Charlie.

Tim clutched his friend's arm. He felt a tear trickle down his cheek. "I'm afraid, Charlie! I don't know what to do."

"I don't know what to do either. Don't worry. We'll figure something out. Promised your momma I'd watch out for you. We'll get back. We gotta get back so she won't worry. Besides, I bet my momma's worried too. All by herself in a storm. We'll get back safe. We'll figure this out together. Right?"

"Right. We'll figure it out. Together," said Tim.

Chapter 16

NOT ALONE

T HE CAVE ENTRANCE AND the dark water below were barely visible. It was early sunrise. The wind had calmed a bit. Although the storm abated, the water continued swirling, lapping against the cave's wall. It looked like it had gone down a little. Only a little.

A tangle of branches lay trapped near the entrance. A large hemlock limb floated below. Charlie pointed the flashlight toward it, illuminating the flattened sprays of small twigs spread out in the water, like tiny hands helping it swim as it bobbed and rocked its way around the cave.

Tim focused on the water and debris, silently contriving various plans for escape.

That's a good-sized branch. Big enough to grab and swim alongside. Betcha it'd get us outta here, and we'd—

Charlie grabbed Tim's arm, interrupting his thought. "Did you hear that?"

"No. What was it?"

"Listen!" Charlie whispered.

"Wha—"

"Shh! There it is again!"

Tim glared at his friend. He didn't like being shushed. Like Uncle Sal telling him to be quiet. Anyway, he heard nothing.

"There! Did you hear that?" asked Charlie.

Was Charlie playing games? Tim took a quick breath. "Nothing! I heard nothing. You're making it up."

"No, I heard something in the water."

Glancing down at the water, Tim felt a panic creeping over him. "What-what do you think it is?"

"Don't know. Shh. Listen. Over that way."

"All I heard was a plop, and a splash," said Tim.

"That's it. Something is in the water," whispered Charlie.

Tim froze at the idea. Something? Some animal? What? In the cave with us? His eyes darted about the water.

He heard it again! Close by. Both focused on its origin, hoping to discover what was in the cave with them.

"Dad," Tim whispered, "help us. Please. Come back."

Charlie turned to Tim. "What did you say?"

"Nothing. Just talking to Dad. I want Dad."

Charlie placed a hand on Tim's shoulder. "It's okay being scared. I know what's out there."

"What is it? Can't be bats. They fly."

"Take it easy. I never seen a bat swim. I bet it's that giant bullfrog we saw yesterday. Remember? The darnedest, biggest bullfrog I ever seen! Wo-o-o-we!"

"You think so? Yeah. Sounds like a frog jumping in and out of the water, don't it? It has to be the bullfrog! He's getting breakfast." Tim giggled, sucking in a shaky breath. "After that giant storm, *he's* looking for breakfast."

Charlie nodded and grinned.

"Give him some Kool-Aid. Heard it tastes great with flies and water bugs," said Tim with a chuckle.

Watching the light slowly increasing at the mouth of the cave, Tim wondered when the water would go away? "You think we'll be out soon?"

"Soon? Yeah, soon. Things will work out okay. We'll get home. Soon," said Charlie.

Tim was relieved. Kind of.

His twenty-four-hour plan to find the bear proved to be a disaster. He *had* to find it. But how? It certainly wasn't possible from the cave's shelf with all that water. Would they get off this shelf later in the morning? Maybe it would take hours for the water to go down. Days? His one chance to find the bear was slipping away. He'd have to come back. Try again.

But, would Charlie come a second time?

Chapter 17

SHARING DREAMS

SCRUNCHED UP ON THEIR blankets, the boys leaned against the makeshift backrest. The rising sun slowly illuminated the cave's entrance, but due to the height of their shelf in the farther part of the cave's entrance, they were still in shadow.

Charlie whispered, "Ain't nothing wrong 'bout missing your poppa. Momma says, 'Just never forget. Be glad you got to know him.' That's what you gotta remember."

Tim mulled over Charlie's words. "Yeah? Guess I'm lucky. Dad and me doing things together. All them memories. But, sometimes thinking about him tears me up. And *that* makes me angry. I *hate* crying. Wish he'd just pop in and say, 'So, how's my boy?'" Uncomfortable at telling his secrets, Tim sneaked a glance at Charlie. "That sound silly?"

"Silly? Nah. When I dream 'bout Poppa, we talk. He teaches me things," whispered Charlie.

Tim sat up. "He does?"

"Yeah."

He never asked Charlie about Mr. Wallace. Mom said it was impolite. But Charlie seemed okay with talking about him. "What does he teach you?"

"Oh, lots of stuff. I may not remember everything when I wake up. But when I need to know something," he tapped his forefinger at his temple, "it's there. In my head. It's like he tells me how to figure things out and stores it in my brain."

"But you're smart. You know how to do all kinds of stuff, and solve problems. No one is there to tell you. Are you sure it ain't you talking to you? You know what I mean? Some people have in-tui-tui-tion."

"Intuition," said Charlie with a smirk.

"That's what I said. Mom told me about that. She has lots of that."

"In-tu-i-tion?" said Charlie.

"Yeah, like I said. She has lots of it."

Charlie chuckled. "Maybe you did. But I *don't* know *everything*. Poppa *has* to be telling me how to do stuff. How to figure things out. It's him telling me. Somehow."

"You think so?"

"Absolutely."

Since Charlie had dreams like that, Tim shared a bit more. "I dreamed about a frog last night, and I talked to him."

"Did it talk back?"

"Yeah. His name is Salubrious Frog!"

"Who? Salu— *He* has a name too? Do all critters you dream about have names?"

Tim shrugged his shoulder. "Don't know. But his name is Salubrious Frog! He's a *giant* frog. His eyes change color, he changes size, and he's very smart. He calls me 'Sir.' He called you 'Sir Charlie!'"

"Slow down some. A giant frog talked to you? About what?"

"Yeah. Listen."

"You gotta be kid—"

"Wait. I'll tell you. I believe Tiny Bear can help us out of here. We need to find him like Dad did. Tiny Bear is here. I know he is. So I asked Salubrious Frog to help find Tiny Bear. But he wouldn't, and he went away. And, I think, almost for sure, I *saw* the bear in the shadows.

"Aw-w, don't be harebrained, Tomata! How can a bear come in here with the flood down there? Was he swimming?"

"It's true, Charlie! On the cave wall. I saw the bear's shape last night.

"Shape?"

"Yeah. At first, with the lightning, I saw all kinds of shapes on the cave wall."

"Oh, you mean silhouettes. Like you see in clouds. Sometimes you see rabbits, angels—"

"Yeah. Silhouettes. They disappeared after a second." Tim snapped his fingers for emphasis. "But the *bear* stayed longer. He nodded his head and waved his paw. I waved back. After that, I fell asleep. That's when Salubrious Frog showed up."

"Are you sure the silhouettes weren't part of your dream?"

"No! They weren't. I'm sure of it."

"Okay. Go on."

With a rush of words, Tim described his dream about Salubrious Frog.

Staring at Tim, Charlie leaned back against the wall, rubbing the bridge of his nose with his forefinger.

"What do you make of my dream?"

"Salubrious Frog comes from the big bullfrog we saw in the cave yesterday. You turned him into something magical."

"You think so?"

"You say, Tiny Bear waved. Did he talk?"

"No. Don't know if he can."

"Salubrious Frog said you're dishonest. Why do you think he said that?"

Tim choked away a whimper. "Salubrious Frog asked if I was angry with Dad. I-I'm not!"

"It's okay, Tim. I know how you feel. When Poppa died, *I* got pretty angry."

"You were?"

"Oh Yeah. Furious! So was Momma! She wouldn't talk about him. How he died. Not with anybody, including me.

"Then I got angry at *her*. But you know what? I felt alone at home, at school, or wherever I went. I always felt alone. So, I got angrier.

Nobody noticed me. If they did, they didn't understand me. Who wants to be around angry people? Seemed like everybody avoided me.

"Nobody knows why you're angry if you don't explain what's going on. If you keep it inside, it makes you angrier. It goes round and round. Know what I mean?"

Tim nodded slightly.

"I realized I was angry at being alone, and angry at being angry. Round and round some more! I had to let it go. Had to learn to be happy again...without Poppa.

"He died, is all. It wasn't anyone's fault. I had to live with that. So did Momma.

"Now I'm happy remembering when we had him around. I got memories of us doing things together from when I was very young until he died. After he died, bed-time grew hard for me. I'd toss and turn for hours before falling asleep. Still do, sometimes."

Charlie stared down at the shelf where he sat. "I'll tell you a secret I never told Momma. A week after Poppa died, around two o'clock in the morning, a noise from somewhere in the house woke me. I swear it sounded like Poppa shuffling around in his boots. I thought, 'In the kitchen? That ain't possible. He's dead.' Then I heard a cough. Same as when he cleared his throat. Being curious, I tip-toed downstairs to check things out. What would I see? I figured...nothing, Poppa's in the cemetery."

"Were you scared?" said Tim.

"At ten years old? You bet I was. I had goosebumps. Standing on that last step, at the bottom of the stairs, holding my breath, I peeked around the corner into the kitchen."

"You see anything?"

"Nothing! The fire in the wood stove crackled, warming the kitchen. I went to the parlor and sat on the sofa, waiting."

"For what?" Tim asked.

"Yeah, that's what I asked myself. 'For what?' I don't know why, but I waited. Next morning, Momma tapped my shoulder, waking me. I didn't want to make her unhappy or worry her, so I said, 'Morning. Kept your fire going for you, Momma.' After touching the stove, she said, 'What fire? I didn't light a fire last night. But I think you need to stoke it again.' She smiled kinda funny at me. I think she figured I started the fire, which I didn't, and she probably thought I missed Poppa and couldn't sleep.

"After that night, I often think he's still around. That he started the fire. How could that be? I don't know. But you know what? I like it that way. It makes me think he came to say 'Goodbye' so I could be peaceful and he kept me warm. The fire? That was Poppa. I didn't understand that until a year later. That's when I stopped being angry."

"Did your mom stop being angry?"

"Like I said, she wouldn't speak about it. It took about three months for her to talk about Poppa. But I was too angry, going round and round and not listening. Now we have long talks about him. We laugh. We cry."

"Your mom cries? Dad cried once. Grown-ups do cry. Crying doesn't mean you're a baby, does it?" said Tim.

"Nope. Like I said, grown-ups don't *like* to cry. They try hard to control it. Guess it ain't mature to cry."

Tim remembered his experience at school with his friends after Dad died. He felt invisible because the kids didn't hang around him much. He hadn't realized why, and that made him angry. Now he understood how Charlie felt, because he often felt the same way.

Charlie's mouth turned upward in a smile, not a cheerful smile, but a weak, sad smile. Moving his gaze toward the water, he said, "I loved Poppa. Still do. He's special no matter where he is. I visit him at the cemetery whenever I have free time."

"I visit Dad at the cemetery too," said Tim.

"Are you sure you're not angry at your poppa?" asked Charlie.

Frowning, Tim smoothed his hair back. He blinked away a tear. "No. I ain't angry at Dad. But Salubrious Frog said I was angry at someone."

Charlie's question struck a chord in Tim's heart. He didn't want to talk about it anymore. It made him sad. Charlie said nothing further. They sat staring at the swirling water in the half-lit cave. The water lapped about, causing the trapped hemlock limb to bob and sway as it traveled round and round inside the cave. Just like Charlie's story about being angry. Then they heard a plop. And a splash.

Chapter 18

NO WATER

IM TOSSED A ROCK into the water. "When will the water go down again?"

Charlie shrugged his shoulders. "Let's hope it's soon. Hey, what's left in the lunchbox?"

Tim was hungry earlier, but his focus on Tiny Bear, going back home, and thoughts of how much time it would take for the water to recede to the riverbed had distracted him.

Mom's pancakes came to mind. Butter melted on top, swimming in a pool of syrup; the last of Grandfather Saunders' supply of maple syrup. Tim's stomach expressed approval with a low growl.

"We're stuck with all this water below us. I'm starving and we're running out of food. We're trapped! We gotta get out of here. We just gotta!" said Tim, with his hands atop his head, as if to keep that thought in his brain.

Charlie placed his hand on Tim's shoulder. "Don't panic. We're safe here! The water will go away! Let's check what we have for food." He retrieved the lunchbox and with the flashlight, he inspected its contents. "We have two peanut butter and jelly sandwiches, one, two, three, um-m, eight good-sized oatmeal cookies, two apples. And a little Kool-Aid. That's it. Not much, is it? It'll have to do."

"No more Hydrox?" said Tim.

"Ate 'em all yesterday."

"Hey! We have lots of water! Dad said people can survive without food for three weeks. Without water, they die in three or four days."

"Can't drink that water. It'll make you sick."

"We can filter it. Put a blanket in the water and wring it out. The junk will get trapped in the blankets, like when I use a strainer to get rid of stuff that gets in Daisy's milk before we pour it in the milk can. We'd have clean water. River water is like regular water. We just need to strain it out some," said Tim.

"But you sterilize the milk pails and milk cans before you milk a cow. And you get pure milk. We can't sterilize our thermos. River water ain't clean. The water has things you can see in it and tons of stuff you *can't* see in it. And you don't even know what most of it *is*. Wish I could tell you different. But after a flood, it sure ain't safe to drink river water," said Charlie.

"If it's polluted after we filter, we'll taste it. We can spit it out," said Tim.

Charlie shut the lunchbox. "Sorry. No! If it's spring water, or water flowing through moss in the woods, then it'd be fine. But river water? Momma says you can't drink it 'less you boil it first. And we don't have a stove, matches, or a pot to boil the water, so we can't drink this water. It'll make us sick."

"It ain't fair for it to be so close and we can't have any," said Tim in a high pitch. "What are we gonna do? How about we jump in and grab that big hemlock branch? We can hang on and swim alongside outta here."

"Thought about that. Too dangerous. With the river moving like it is inside the cave, it's probably moving faster outside the cave. We could get dragged under water or too far downriver. Things floating downriver could smash into us. Terrible things could happen. We'll sit and wait. Poppa used to say, if you're lost, stay put and wait. If you move around, chances are nobody will find you," said Charlie.

"Dad said that, too. You think someone will find us?"

"Sure! Your uncle and our mommas are looking for us right now!"

A spark of hope came over Tim.

"Seeing the little food we have, we'll eat a tiny bit once a day till they find us, and—"

"A tiny bit? Once a day?" Tim's hope slipped into the unclean water below.

"Yeah, we gotta figure how long we'll be stranded here. My guess is one or two days—"

"Stranded? Two days?" Tim's loud, cracked squeak echoed through the cave.

"Maybe. Maybe not. We may be out in a few hours. Or minutes. We'll be *okay*. Just calm *down*. Getting worked up don't help and won't get us anywhere." Charlie set the lunchbox back behind the knapsack.

Tim stared at the knapsack hiding the lunchbox they had packed with food before leaving. He remembered how they had enjoyed their meal the night before. If only they hadn't eaten so much. But how could they know they'd have to weather a storm in a cave without starving? Or dying of thirst?

Squinting into the dimness, he wondered if Tiny Bear was in the cave. *I know that was him last night.*

"Tiny Bear! Please help us. We need your help!" he shouted.

Charlie turned with a start. "Did you see something?"

Tim shook his head. "Nah. Thought maybe Tiny Bear was here. Did I scare you?"

"You surprised me. You figure maybe he's watching us?"

"My imagination's working overtime. We'll get home again, won't we?"

"We sure will. Don't you worry. We'll be home soon." This time, Charlie's reassuring words persuaded Tim that rescue could be possible. Soon.

Chapter 19

UNCLE SAL

Before sunrise, Uncle Sal Saunders headed home from a North Conway motel where he stayed during the previous night's hurricane. Within ten miles travel, Route 16 South was blocked by downed trees, and an electrical pole lay with its snapped wires on the wet pavement.

So he turned back, searching for a back road. Even though the road he chose was muddy from the hurricane's rainfall, he successfully drove to the outskirts of Conway Village. He planned to cross the Village Road Bridge spanning the Saco River as a detour back to Route 16 South.

As he approached the bridge entrance, he swerved to avoid a fallen tree. His rear wheel struck a rock and dropped into the depression left by that rock. Immediately, his two rear wheels spun, drilling themselves down into the mud.

Piled-up tree limbs, a pine tree, and a section of roof from a coop or a well lay pressed against damaged bridge supports now barely visible beneath the water.

Craning his neck, he inspected the sky through the truck's windshield. Remains of gloomy gray clouds moved east. Early light revealed the hurricane's destruction. Mangled trees bent down as if searching for relatives lost in the murky water.

Sal groaned. "How'm I gonna get home?" He worried his farm might have been in the hurricane's path. "Oh, let the farm be okay."

He shifted the gear into forward and reverse, rocking his truck back and forth. But the wheels only spun themselves deeper. Rocking worked in snow and ice. But in mud? Useless. The truck had now sunk to its rear axle. "Road swallowed my wheels," he mumbled.

He stepped out, and the soupy mud grabbed his leather boots. "Ah, *gee*. My best boots. Ruined for sure!"

In drier conditions, Sal's farmhouse was about a three-hour walk from the bridge. Walking across the bridge at this time was not an option, for it could collapse at any moment. Pulling his straw hat down to his ears, he decided to follow the river's edge. He'd follow it, heading south toward Conway Village, and cross to the other side at a bend he knew to be the most narrow area between the opposite banks, where he'd follow the Saco going east to River Fork.

Sal picked up a limb resembling an over-sized walking stick for support. From his truck, he retrieved his heavy duty logging rope from under the seat. The rope had a small wooden block attached on one end to lead the rope through the air whenever Uncle Sal threw it up over a limb to climb a tree.

Keeping an eye out for large floating objects moving downstream with the current, Sal prodded and waded along the swollen edge of the river. He climbed over downed trees and stumbled over submerged, slippery rocks. At one point, he got entangled in unseen underwater branches. He used his stick to poke the muddy ground, or to float, which helped him swim free. Other times, he'd rope a branch or anything solid ahead of him to pull himself forward. After nearly an hour of wading, he felt his heart pounding hard. Gasping for breath, he chided himself, "Give it a rest. No sense rushing."

He sat on a half submerged guardrail to calm his heart and regain his breath.

Once rested, he continued on until he finally reached that narrow bend. Well, it used to be narrow.

Taking a chance, he entered the river and made it to the other side by swimming across a bit, and letting the current carry him as he gripped his stick and rope. The current provided swift travel downriver until he reached shallow water at the opposite bank. Unfortunately, he had traveled farther downriver, beyond his farm.

From there, Sal walked for nearly half an hour to his farmhouse. Drained of energy, his body ached. The joints in his hands, legs, and feet were stiff. Every muscle objected to having worked so hard, demanding, "Why the rush?" Another night in a motel and coming home after the storm would have been easier.

At home, Sal found his porch steps under water. The screen door had broken like a matchstick against the porch railing.

With its roof missing and its door floating nearby, the tool shed was flooded.

Sitting in several inches of water, the barn door remained shut. The hens inside cackled. Tom, the rooster, crowed. It was time to rise, time to be fed, and Sal was late.

Sal called to his flock, "Chick, chick, chi-i-ick!"

The hens quieted.

Tom crowed.

"I'll feed you in a bit!" Sal called out.

He entered the farmhouse with caution. Stepping inside, he slapped his leg and smiled. "You made it, girl! You made it. I'm no religious guy, but I need to thank the Lord for sparing my old farmhouse. And me."

Though the living quarters were dry, the basement had flooded. Sal figured about two feet of water. "Lots of work. Nothing I can't fix." He stepped back upstairs and closed the basement door.

From the second-story bedroom window, he surveyed the whole of his farm. A downed tree fell away from the front porch. Scattered branches lay across the porch roof below, where roofing shingles were now missing. The barn's metal roof needed attention. Two of its metal sections floated in the orchard. Another metal strip, hanging on by a few nails, had peeled back like a page half torn from an open book.

He stepped into the bathroom. A large tree branch had blown through the window. Glass and water covered the floor. He returned to the bedroom to get towels from the linen closet to sop up the water.

Could have been worse. Hurricanes make a heck of a mess. Haven't had a bad hurricane in decades.

He made a mental note of the damage. *Crops gone. Barn and house need fixing. And the well! It'll take a while to clean that out.*

Gotta call Nel. See how she and Tim are doing? Their farm is northeast of the river, beyond a ridge. Perhaps the ridge protec—

"Oh, no! The boys!" Sal had forgotten his promise to Nel. He ran downstairs and grabbed the wall phone from its receiver.

No dial tone! It's dead!

Get to Nel's! No.

Go to the campsite first. Just in case. Then go to Nel's!

Let them not have gone to the river. Or at least, let them have returned home okay.

Racing upstairs, he repeated at every breath, "Let-them-be-safe, let-them-be-safe, let-them-be-safe!" Rapid repetition aloud was his way of wishing for something to happen. Like crossing one's fingers.

He stripped off his wet clothes, snapped dry clothing out of the closet with hangers flipping off the rod, landing at his feet. His fly-fishing boots, stored deep in the closet's rear, would be good to wear. He quickly slipped them on and buttoned his shirt as he rushed to the barn.

Stiff from his journey home, he strained to prop two old eight foot planks across two wooden barrels, creating a platform up off the barn's floor. Scooping feed from the metal bin, he filled feeding pans and spare pails and placed them onto the platform. Tom, the rooster, eager for his late breakfast, flew up onto the new platform. The hens followed.

"Best I can do. Make it last. I'll be gone for a long while. Tom, take care of your ladies."

Sal clambered up the hayloft ladder. Pulling at ropes threaded through two pulleys, he lowered the rowboat with its oars, suspended from the barn's high rafters onto the flooded barn floor.

His brother, Wes, had designed and installed a pulley system for Sal to store the boat above, out of the way. This was the first time Sal made use of it. Pleased with the ease of lowering the boat and its equipment, he smiled up at the barn's rafters. *Nice job, Wes.*

Sal steered the boat outside the barn. After sliding the door shut, he stepped into his boat and rowed toward the river, heading for the campsite to check on Tim and Charlie!

Chapter 20

STRANDED

"TWEE, TWEE-EE-EE," A HAWK's high-pitched call awakened Roach as it landed on the slope above her. To her amazement, it landed on a protruding root above where she lay. Groggy from lack of sleep, she watched the bird turn around and around on its precarious perch, all the while keeping an eye on her, cocking its head side-to-side.

"Shoo. Go away!" Roach shook her free arm at the bird. "Shoo, shoo! Go on! Go!"

It pivoted, bobbed its head, and kept its eyes on Roach.

"What are you doing? You'll get dizzy and fall in the mud, like me!"

She ignored the bird, but after a while, her curiosity challenged her not to peek. So, she peeked.

Why was it still there? "It's impolite to stare. Shoo!"

The bird didn't move.

In the dim sunrise, Roach surveyed the slope from her root cradle to its granite ledge far below. Mud had flowed down the slope and beyond, over the ledge.

"Holy cow!" she said aloud. She shuddered. She could have easily slipped into the river during the storm! Luck was certainly on her side.

She poked her fingers into the mud, exploring for something solid to grab hold of. "It's too wet to climb." She turned to the hawk. "Hey bird? I can use some help here. Please?"

The hawk spread its large wings, flew off, splaying its wing tips like fingers.

"No! Don't. Don't go!"

It landed further down the slope on a large root sticking out of the mud.

"You found another root!"

Again, it flew up and landed on a second, larger root further down, and there were more.

Roach had a way down. The hawk was helping her! "Animals *can't* talk, but if you pay attention, they certainly have something to say! I don't know hawk-talk, but we're talking, aren't we?

"Boy, Mrs. Stark's sure won't believe it when I tell her about me talking with a hawk!"

The hawk bobbed its head twice, flew up, and landed on a large damaged hemlock barely visible above the top of the muddy slope that Roach had slipped down.

"Bird! Come back!"

Keeping an eye on the hawk and focusing on the roots protruding from the slope, Roach crept out of her cradle. Rolling onto her belly, she inched her way down in a slow, slippery crawl, feet first, to the next root. Though she slid a little, it didn't scare her. The hawk was there to protect her. Every time she reached a root, she waved at her new friend. The hawk bobbed its head in return.

At the last root, she squealed: "I made it! I made it! Thank you, beautiful hawk!"

"Twee, twee-ee-ee, twee-ee-ee," the hawk responded. It circled overhead and flew away.

Roach stood on the muddy ledge overlooking the trees below. The river had swelled over its banks into the forest.

Touching her hair, she found it gritty and caked with mud. Her skin, clothing, and shoes were muddied and wet.

She searched the sky. "Hawk! Where are you? And *where* am *I*? How will I get out of here?"

The sky slowly brightened, revealing three shades of blue, with a scattering of fluffy clouds drifting north. Below her, the brown water carried uprooted trees, broken limbs and other debris downriver.

Roach cautiously paced the granite ledge to avoid slipping into the river.

"So much water!" she whispered.

She'd climb up the slope after it dried a bit.

Meanwhile, she worried about her friends. Had they escaped?

Please let them be okay.

Charlie. He don't even know I— Oh, will I see him again?

And Tim?

I gotta find them!

"Hawk where are you? Come back. I need to find my friends!"

She searched the sky, stepping as close to the edge as she dared to peek beyond a rocky outcropping blocking her view. The hawk had vanished.

Roach sat away from the edge, surveying the river. Would she, Charlie, and Tim get back home?

Though the day brightened, Roach's spirit did not. She ached from clutching the cradle all night. And she realized she was very, very hungry. She wanted to get home to Gram's. But first, she had to find her friends.

She needed a plan, but no ideas came to her. Soon, staying awake grew harder to do, so she gave up planning and stretched out on the warming granite ledge.

The debris floated downriver with a rhythm that lulled her tired body to relax. The rising sun warmed her, and she dozed off. In a much needed sleep, she caressed her mother's red crystal necklace and dreamed of the time Lizbet had given it to her.

"*Here, Roachelle, sweetie, wear my necklace. My favorite. Wear it every day until I come back for you.*"

"*When will you come back?*"

Lizbet paused. "I don't know. Soon. I promise." She stepped into the back of a black car, and it drove away.

Roach chased the car, shouting, "Take me too! Don't go!"

But the car continued down Dodge Hill Road and vanished at the switchback.

Nearby, Sal struggled with floating debris passing him as he rowed downriver in his boat, calling, "Tim! Charlie! Anybody there?"

Deep in sleep, Roach didn't hear his call.

Chapter 21

THE SEARCH

DETERMINED TO REACH HIS destination, Sal carefully rowed with the current, which appeared to have slowed a bit. He diverted floating debris and tree limbs that came his way with his oars. Arriving at the campsite, he shouted, "Tim! Charlie! Anybody there? Hello!"

Nobody answered.

Perhaps the boys were safe at home.

The river flowed high above the banking, and the lean-to was gone. Trees without tops resembled sticks placed at odd angles in the water. Other trees were uprooted. The upper trunk of a giant hemlock near the river had exploded. Its branches lay scattered at the base of the rocky outcropping near the campsite.

The boys must be home!

Sal paddled his way to the edge of the Lower Wood. The sun peeked through the clouds and warmed his back as he hopped out and dragged the boat ashore, tying it to a tree.

He plodded up through the woods toward Nel's farm. Because of the hurricane, he kept alert for possible widow makers—uprooted or cut trees and limbs left snagged in the upper canopy—which could later drop without warning on unsuspecting travelers below. That's what happened to Spencer Wallace, Charlie's father.

One winter evening Spencer stopped to pick up his logging tools, and a limb dropped. Late that night, Wes, Sal, and Lila found his body covered in the newly fallen snow. The next morning, Wes helped Lila make funeral arrangements with the undertaker. Later that afternoon, Wes drove home in a torrent of tears for losing Spencer, his long-time friend.

Sal continued next through the upper ridge and through the Old Wood, arriving at its outer edge, overlooking Nel's farmhouse. In the field were Nel and Lila.

Nel's okay! She got some pretty soggy field from the look of it. But the farmhouse looks okay.

He called out, waved, and jogged over to them. Both women ran, meeting Sal halfway.

With a note of alarm in her voice, Nel said, "Where's Tim! Where's Charlie!"

Sal stopped short. "They're not with you? Oh, God!" Removing his hat, he smoothed his hair back. His face turned crimson. "I'm so ashamed. I-I didn't check on the boys like I promised."

"Why not!" demanded Nel.

"I'm so, so sorry. I got stranded in North Conway last night. I left early this morning, but my truck got stuck at the Conway's Village Road bridge. So I followed the river on foot and crossed it by floating downstream with the current. The boys weren't at the farm. So I rowed to the camp site. The boat is still tied down at the Lower Wood."

"Oh God! Oh, no! Tim and Charlie are still out there?" wailed Nel. All color drained from her face.

With her eyes opened wide and tears trickling down her cheeks, Lila covered her mouth with both hands.

"Since they weren't at the campsite, I figured they made their way home by now," said Sal.

"I can't go through this again," said Nel, her voice shaking. She grabbed her brother-in-law's shirt and buried her face into it. "No, no-o!"

Sal's throat tightened, tears trickled down his cheeks as he held Nel's arms. "I'll go search again. If I don't see them, I'll go back home to double check, they could be there now. We may have missed each other. But first, we need help from the sheriff's office."

Lila's eyes met Sal's. A strangled cry emerged from her throat. Tears streamed down her cheeks. Her hands shaking, she grabbed Nel's shoulder and turned her around. The women hugged.

Nel pulled away, wiped her tears with her palms, and fought to calm herself. With a quavering voice, and her eyes shut tight, she announced, "We have to go back to the river to find the boys."

"Yes! Of course. We'll find them. We can cover more ground together," said Sal.

"Right," said Nel. "Let's try the phone again. Maybe we'll get through to the sheriff this time!"

Back inside the farmhouse, Nel picked up the phone's receiver. "Nothing. The line's down somewhere."

"I'll go to Gram's. See if her phone works. I'll check on her and Roachelle at the same time. You go with Sal. I'll catch up with you," said Lila as she ran out the door.

Sal and Nel hurried back over the field and through the Old Wood. As they approached the upper ridge, neither spoke. Both knew what the other thought: "Where are the boys?"

Chapter 22

TINY BEAR

THE MORNING SUNLIGHT TRICKLED in, dimly lighting the cave. Its beams danced on the swirling water below. The hemlock limb, now visible, bobbed and swayed.

"Was Salubrious Frog right?" Tim thought out loud.

"About what?" said Charlie.

"About me being angry? He said Dad left me and Mom. But he didn't, he died. It ain't fair. He wasn't supposed to die until he got old."

Charlie thought about Tim's words. "You can't predict when someone is supposed to die. And yes, it ain't ever fair when someone does die. But there's nothing we can do to change that."

"My friend at school, his grandfather died in a hospital. Then he wasn't dead anymore. He came back! I want Dad to come back! I want—"

"I know what you want. I'd like the same for me. It took a long time for me to accept that it happened. That it was *supposed* to happen."

"'Supposed to happen?' He was '*supposed*' to be my dad, and he was '*supposed*' to be a grandfather someday, like my Grandfather Saunders. Why did he die? Why are we born if we all die, anyway?" asked Tim.

"Your poppa was here, so *you* could be here. Mine was here, so *I* could be here. Listen, you have pictures. Memories. Remember his touch, his laugh, and his funny stories, like that story about Tiny Bear."

"It's not a '*funny*' story. Tiny Bear is real! He's *real*. Dad said so. He saw it. Tiny Bear will get us out of here. I *know* he will. And he can bring Dad back. He *has* to!"

Tim crossed his arms and legs. "Jeepers! I loved Dad. I miss him *so* much. Why did he have to die? It ain't *fair. Dang it!* It ain't!" He wiped away an oncoming tear.

"Here, take this," said Charlie, retrieving the blood-stained handkerchief from his pocket. "It's never fair. Maybe your poppa talked to you through that hawk. I mean, maybe that was your dad, not the hawk, saying, 'Hello,' or 'Watch out for the river.'

"Understand what I'm saying? Maybe he talks to you in your dreams. Could be he tried to tell you if you stop being angry at him for leaving, for dying, you'd see Tiny Bear. Like Momma says, 'You gotta let it go.'"

"You think so?" Tim's voice wobbled. "You think Dad's talking to me?"

"Strange things are true, sometimes. And you gotta let it go so you can go on with your life. That's what Momma says. So, don't just cry for your pap—"

"I ain't *crying*! Babies cry. I'm almost thirteen. I ain't a baby."

"You said your poppa cried in his truck. He wasn't a baby either. He protected you from his sadness. He didn't tell you why he cried that day. He wanted you to be happy. You wanna disappoint him?"

"No," whispered Tim. He stared at the bobbing limb.

"Your momma said Uncle Sal loves you. Maybe he does! Why don't *you* like him? Is it because you're angry at *him*? I wish I had an Uncle Sal. Say! What's that frog's name?"

"Salubrious Frog."

"Maybe that was your Uncle *Sal*ubrious. Get it? Salubrious, Uncle Sal–ubrious Frog? Listen; maybe you need your uncle's help to find Tiny Bear." Charlie leaned back against the wall. "Anyway, I think that's what the dream of you in the river was about. To not be angry. You gotta let it go."

"Gosh. Maybe— Maybe you're right. It would be nice to have Uncle Sal on my side. But sometimes he's scary. Salubrious Frog was kinda scary, too. He said I was angry. Angry at who? Uncle Sal? Mom? Both of them? But not at Dad, he's de—" Tim's throat tightened. Speech became difficult. After a few moments, he recovered his voice.

"Maybe you're right about Dad. Grandfather Saunders died, and Grandmother died a few years later. Afterward, Dad talked about the fun times they all shared. When he talked about them, sometimes he'd laugh. Yeah, maybe Dad wants me to be happy. He always took care of me. That made him happy. I'm not angry at Dad. Just...sad.

"Sal-ubrious Frog. Uncle Sal. Coming down that tree. Those eyes, those whiskers. Promise not to tell Uncle Sal I dreamed he was a giant frog!"

Both laughed. Their laughter echoed up from the water along the cave walls.

"I'm hungry, are you?" asked Tim.

"Yeah, but we can wait. We'll be fine. Tiny Bear will help us out of here."

"*You* think so, *too*?" Tim smiled from ear to ear. "Yeah, we need to make a wish. I wish Mom and Uncle Sal to be safe from the storm. I wish Charlie's mom safe from the storm. Roach and Gram, I wish them safe from the storm."

"Roach? What made you think of her?"

"I don't know. She visits a lot. Lives alone with Gram. She's kinda like us."

"Why do you say that?"

"Because her mom's gone. Been gone a long time. When Roach visits us, she swears her mom is coming home soon. But it's been two years. I wonder if she'll ever come back."

"That long?"

"Yeah. And when Roach visits, she asks lots of questions about you. I tell her 'ask him yourself.'"

"Ask what?"

"Stuff like, if you know a lot of girls her age?"

"She goes to River Fork High. She must have girlfriends at school. Why come to me looking for friends?" said Charlie.

"That's what I wondered. Guess maybe she's lonely and wants to meet other girls. There aren't too many around our neighborhood."

Charlie shook his head. "Think Tiny Bear can handle that many wishes?"

"He can handle anything. But you gotta listen."

"To what?" asked Charlie.

"If you hear him laugh, your wishes will come true."

"How about us? Don't forget—"

"I wish Charlie, Blackberry Head, be safe from the storm. I ain't supposed to wish for myself."

"Okay. So, I wish Tim, Tomata Head, be safe from the storm." Charlie chuckled and mussed Tim's hair. They giggled, not a loud giggle, yet the sound echoed off the walls and the water below. They eyed the cave's dark recesses and listened in awe. At first, the echo grew louder and seemed to multiply, surrounding them. The boys huddled closer together, unsure what to do. Slowly, the echo faded with a sigh in the belly of the cave.

Minutes passed, then they heard another plop and a splash. Tim strained his eyes to find the source in the swirling water below.

"Look, Charlie. There." He pointed to the right of the bobbing limb.

"I see it. But I can't believe it. That dang old bullfrog is still here! Look at him go! He's the darnedest, biggest bullfrog I ever seen."

The frog swam to the limb, hopped onto its thick greenery, turned, and faced the boys.

"Hi, frog. Hi, Uncle Sal-ubrious Frog!" said Tim with a chuckle.

"Don't get confused, Tomata," said Charlie. "He's not your uncle, he's just a frog. The darnedest, biggest bullfr— Well, he's a *special* bullfrog."

"Watch! He's doing something," said Tim.

The frog stood on its hind legs and stretched its front legs up midair.

"He did that yesterday!" said Charlie.

"Yeah. Shh!" whispered Tim, his eyes glued to the spectacle.

The frog stood for several seconds, then crouched like a regular frog.

Something moved from behind.

Tim reached out to Charlie and whispered, "Look. See? See?"

"Yea-ah. What *is* it?" said Charlie.

"I don't know."

From the hemlock's thick needles, a creature emerged. It ambled toward the frog, stopped and faced the boys. It stood upright, stretched its paws high, lowered its head, dropped to stand on its four legs, and stood again. Tim pulled and twisted Charlie's shirtsleeve with one hand, pointing with the other.

"Look, Charlie! Do you see? Do you?"

He shook Charlie's sleeve, repeating, "Do you *see* him?"

Charlie hesitated. "Yeah. Yeah. I see. What is that? A bear? The darnedest, smallest bear *I* ever seen!"

"I *told* you he was small. That's Tiny Bear! He did the same thing last night! Just like that. He came to see me! He did! That was him. It's the same as the silhouette.

"Hello! Tiny Bear!" said Tim. "Please help us! We need to get home! Dad said you would help if we needed you! Remember Dad? Wes Saunders! I'm his son, Tim Saunders. We need your help. Please help us out of here!"

The bear lowered its head, dropped, stood for a few more seconds, turned, and vanished into the hemlock's shadows. The boys stared. Would it return?

Several minutes passed. Nothing else happened.

"Tiny Bear's gone. And look, the frog's gone, too! Where did they go?" asked Charlie.

Tim shook his head. "I don't know."

"You think he'll help us?"

"I think so. I hope so," said Tim.

"Man! I never seen anything like it," said Charlie.

"I told you! Dad saw Tiny Bear, now *we* saw him *too*! Not everyone gets to see him. And we heard him laugh! That was the *bear* laughing in the cave a while ago."

"I figured it was him," said Charlie.

Suddenly, a brilliant light made its way through a crevice behind the boys. It traveled across the shelf floor and down onto the water, partially illuminating the bobbing limb.

Charlie tapped Tim's shoulder. "Look! Behind us!"

Tim scrambled on his hands and knees to see. A sunbeam blazed through an opening in the rock. "A tiny hole! We can get out, Charlie. We can get out!"

Quickly clawing at the hole, Charlie loosened the surrounding rock. After pulling out two pieces of loose rock, he stopped.

"What's the matter?" said Tim.

"Don't want rocks falling on us."

"Tiny Bear won't let that happen. You gotta believe that. He's *helping* us!"

After staring at the crevice for a moment, Charlie pushed his fingers through it. "I can feel the air. It's warm. Maybe someone will come. If your uncle comes, and we shout loud enough, he might hear us. Get the flashlight so I can see what I'm doing!"

"Uncle Sal! Yeah, he's supposed to check on us. Maybe he'll come today. Help! Uncle Sal. Help!" shouted Tim.

"Get the flashlight!" said Charlie.

Grabbing the flashlight, Tim lit the crevice and repeatedly yelled, "Uncle Sal! Help!"

Charlie tugged at the wall, pulling out chunks of rock. He used the bigger rocks to hammer at the hole. More stones fell. The opening widened.

Tim's shouts and Charlie's pounding echoed all around them. Whenever a good-sized chunk fell, the boys cheered. The opening grew large enough to reveal treetops and the river below.

"The cave has two entrances!" said Tim.

Chapter 23

SECOND TRY

S AL AND NEL RAN through the Old Wood, following Tim's planned route to get to the Saco. They called out to the boys several times. No one answered. When the Lower Wood stood visible beyond a rocky meadow, Nel burst into tears. "We have to find them. Lord, let them be safe. Bring them home." Tilting her head to the sky, she said, "Dear Wes, help us find Tim and Charlie."

After a pause, Sal said, "Nel, I been thinking. You should go back and stay with Lila 'til I get back. Three adults, sitting in a boat navigating rough waters is dangerous. Adding the two boys will make it more dangerous."

Nel hesitated, then agreed. She immediately headed back, and Sal sprinted through the Lower Wood to the River.

Once he reached his boat, he planned to focus on the higher ground where Tim and Charlie might be stranded. Once in the swollen river, he noticed the water current had slowed down even more. He rowed with renewed caution and debated if he should go back to his farm for the outboard motor.

Better not. It'll take too much time. And I might not hear the boys with a motor chugging away.

Tears welled in Sal's eyes. "Wes," he whispered. "I sure miss you, brother. Nel and Lila need the boys. We need the boys!"

With each pull of his oars, Sal became more determined; he would indeed find the boys.

Desperate to do something, Nel paced her field between the Magic Meadow and the edge of the Old Wood, waiting for Lila. She cried out, "Tim, Charlie, come home. Lila, where are you? Please hurry.

"Wes. Wes, I need you. *We* need you!

"I want you back with me and Tim. I want our Tim back.

"The boys, oh, God! Bring them back!"

Her cheeks burned with salty tears; like in a nightmare, her panic filled voice emerged as a whimper. The inability to control her voice heightened her despair.

"I can't go on without my Tim. God, dear God. Bring the boys back home!"

Breathless from running, Lila returned from Gram's and found Nel kneeling on the muddy ground, crying out in a high-pitched hiss. The wet ground splattered as she slapped it with each cry. Lila pulled her friend up by her shoulders and wrapped her arms around her. The women embraced and wept.

"Sal will find the boys. He'll come home with them. I know he will," said Lila.

Chapter 24

GRAM

M INUTES AFTER LILA RETURNED, an old pickup truck turned off Dodge Hill Road into Nel's driveway. While backfiring, lurching, and leaning from side to side, it turned left onto Nel's open field near the driveway. It got stuck in the mud and got unstuck. Tapping the accelerator, Gram slowly crept forward toward Nel and Lila. Gram was a skillful driver, able to handle every misbehaving antic of her old truck.

Sixteen years earlier, Pa Hallstead took an interest in a neighbor's broken down 1929 Model A pickup. The pickup had been stored inside, at the back of the neighbor's dairy barn. Without telling Gram, Pa spent evenings tinkering with the pickup's engine. Finally, he got it to run "pretty good." The next afternoon, he asked Gram if she'd like to ride around a bit with Ol' Elroy.

"Who's Ol' Elroy?"

Pa grinned. With a twinkle in his eye, he said, "Ol' Elroy? Why, Ol' Elroy is in the yard. Take a look-see."

Gram pulled the kitchen curtain aside and peeked at the driveway. "There ain't no Elroy in the yard. He must a gone somewhere an' left his truck." She turned and found her husband chuckling with his corn-cob pipe clenched between his teeth. "What's goin' on? Tell me this instant, Pa. You hear? This instant!"

"Elroy ain't gone no place. He's right there, he sure is. Elroy's in the yard!"

"That truck? Is Ol' Elroy?"

"Yup. You got it, Ol' Woman."

She walked over to Pa, tapping him on the elbow. "Where's the key, Ol' Man?"

"In the ignition, Ol' Woman." He opened the kitchen door. With his pipe in hand, Pa gave his wife a sweeping bow. She curtsied, raised her chin, and stepped outside to meet Ol' Elroy.

Gram mastered driving Ol' Elroy, no matter the season, or the challenges presented by River Fork's graveled, hilly back-roads and switchbacks, or the truck's frequent mischievous lurches. None of it bothered her.

After Pa died, Gram did what she could to maintain the truck. She parked it in the barn's old horse stable and occasionally drove it to town when necessary or for emergencies—like today. This was definitely an emergency.

Nel and Lila stood in the field next to the Old Wood, watching Gram maneuver her truck through soft spots in Nel's field.

The closer the truck got, the louder the backfire. It would be comical, except for today's situation.

Lila said, "Gram's phone doesn't work either. And Roachelle is missing. Gram hasn't seen her since yesterday morning. She's very worried."

The women rushed to meet Gram as Ol' Elroy's wheels sank several inches into a rut. Gram stepped out onto the running board, her face pale in contrast to her blood-shot eyes. "Roachelle? Where are you?" she said in a whimper.

"Gram!" Nel called as she approached the vehicle. "Leave your truck here. We'll get it out later. What's happened with Roachelle?"

"I don't know. She run off yesterday. Jus' like that. No breakfast either. Been calling and looking for her. I plum wore out my legs lookin' for her all day and during the storm. Where is she? You seen her? Oh Lord. And now Lila tells me your boys are lost! I won't forgive myself if something bad happened to Roachelle," said Gram, somber faced, her voice trembling. "God help us!" She wiped her cheek with her palm and covered her quivering lips.

Lila took Gram's trembling hands. "Did you sleep at all?"

"Not a wink. I don't think you got any sleep either, did you?"

"Here, Gram, sit in your truck," said Nel. "You look exhausted; you need to rest. Sal's gone looking for Tim and Charlie. They left early yesterday, after breakfast. Perhaps Roachelle went with them."

"Think so? Now, that could be. Could be. Breakfast time. That's when she disappeared. Come lookin' for her, I did. Come lookin'."

"If that's so, my Charlie will make sure everyone is safe. Sal's searching for them now. He'll find them and bring them home. Don't fret. The children will be home soon," said Lila.

"You think so? Oh yes, Charlie. Fine boy. Tim. A fine boy, too. Roachelle. O-o-oh, Roachelle is a handful. I'm so tired, and my rheumatism is bad. Gotta rest. I'll sit in Ol' Elroy for a spell. My Roachelle will come home. The boys will too. Won't they, Lila?"

Gram sat back in her truck. Lila reached inside and grabbed the afghan from the passenger seat, tucked it onto Gram's lap, and shut the door. Lila met Nel's gaze from across the hood, and the two women silently turned and headed back to the Old Wood's edge.

Staring out the windshield, Gram murmured, "Where are the children? Oh Lord, help Sal find them." She rested her head against the seat's backrest, dabbing her eyes with the afghan.

Chapter 25

SHADOW-MAN

ALF AWAKE, ROACH NOTICED a man with long white hair standing atop the slope. Was that the shadow-man? Following her? The hawk circled above him.

"Hawk. You came back!" Roach whispered. She blinked. The shadow-man disappeared. Was she dreaming? She was too tired to think further.

The bird swooped down to where she lay, then climbed higher in a circular pattern, disappearing high above. Her eyelids grew heavy, giving way to sleep.

The earth moved.

Or was she floating?

Warmth enveloped her.

Did she slip into the river? Was her body drifting, floating?

The wolf. Where was it now? Had it kept her safe? Was it her friend? Why did she think that?

He picked Roach up and gently cradled her in his arms, carrying her along a trail carved in the forest floor thousands of years ago by his ancestors. He gave thanks for the calm and sunny day and sang an old song learned from his great great grandmother—an Indian lullaby.

His steps were swift, smooth, and silent. Animals didn't run away. They paused in recognition, respecting his presence, for they all shared the same forest.

On the riverbank, in a clearing, his wife tended a pot set over a fire pit. Her clothing resembled his. Her skin tone appeared lighter, and her long white hair was tied back.

Noticing his arrival, she rose to greet him. "What have you brought, Husband?"

"A child lost in a storm. She is very tired. We must care for her."

"I will prepare a bed," said the wife. In the wigwam, she placed a mat of woven bulrush onto the ground, away from the interior fire pit, and covered the mat with a handwoven blanket. The husband gently placed Roach onto the bedding, and the wife tucked another blanket over her.

"Poor child."

"I go now to find the other children," said the husband.

"I know you will find them. Makazawigek Siômo will be with you."

The old Indian smiled and walked away along the Saco River. His ancestors had once known this as the land Great Spirit provided. His bare feet, unaffected by cold, snow, rain, and slippery paths, pressed into the coolness of the earth.

Making his way through the woods, he looked up at the hawk flying above. "Ah, Makazawigek Siômo, you be with me. Guide me to the mannanékkañn, the lost boys. We will help them."

Chapter 26

UNCLE SAL PRAYS

S AL BATTLED THE RAIN-SWOLLEN current, as he paddled up and down river, pulling fiercely at his oars, to avoid being dragged away from the campsite.

He peered into the woods along the river's edge, wondering if the boys were hanging on a tree limb or walking at a higher ground. Or had they made it to his farm after he left for Nel's? These thoughts went round and round.

For half an hour, Sal rowed and called out, "Tim! Charlie! Hello! It's Uncle Sal! Can you hear me? Hello!" There was no response.

Boys wouldn't be here this long after a hurricane. Please, please let them have found shelter. But where?

A dull ache spread from Sal's upper arms to his lower back.

"I'll check the farm again, Wes. Hope they arrived after I left."

Save your strength. If they're not there, get the outboard. Ah, but they must *be at the farm!*

Pulling hard at his oars, going upstream, Sal finally made it back to his farm.

Once home, he called out again and again, listening for any distant sound; perhaps a muffled cry for help?

Nothing.

He tied his boat to the porch, calling, "Hello? Anybody here?"

Again, nothing.

He entered his farmhouse, checking every room to be certain the boys hadn't heard his call because they were asleep.

Nobody was inside.

Back outside, he pulled the boat to the barn, calling as he waded across the yard.

Recognizing Sal's voice, Tom crowed louder and louder. The hens added their angry cackles, demanding to be let out.

Sal's shoulders slumped. His vision blurred as unexpected weeping and grief shook his whole being.

He moaned, "Wes. Brother. Where *are* the boys?"

He took a deep breath and exhaled noisily through his closed lips, and brushed away his tears. "Gotta focus. Be in control. Focus, focus! Find the boys!"

Securing the boat at the barn entrance, he slid the barn door on its track just enough to step in. Once inside, he waded across the barn floor and climbed up to the loft where he stored his father's old 1939 Johnson outboard motor.

With the overhead pulleys, Sal lowered the motor from the loft, letting it hover just above the barn floor. He raced down the ladder, grabbed the motor, untied it and carried it to the boat. His sore muscles protested as he carried the forty-two pound outboard across the wet and slick wooden surface beneath his feet. Relieved at not stumbling, he mounted the outboard onto the boat's transom.

Sal checked the motor, added oil and gas, and tucked a spare fuel can beneath the seat upon which three hens now sat, expecting a handout.

He snatched the stray hens and tossed them upward into the barn. Each squawked and awkwardly landed on the plank beside the rooster. They cackled angrily at Sal, reminding him they were hungry!

He grabbed the feed bucket, filled it with more grain, and placed it on the board for the hens to feast.

Once outside, he shut the barn door, untied the boat, climbed in, and with the oar, pushed the boat away from the farmyard to the river's deeper water before starting its motor. His plan: return to the campsite, then head to Nel's with the boys.

Taking a deep breath, he sent a prayer and a request to his brother to help find Tim and Charlie.

Chapter 27

CHARLIE'S DILEMMA

CHARLIE'S JAW TIGHTENED, HIS eyes squinted as he pulled and hammered at the opening. When a rock loosened from the cave wall's stubborn hold, he exhaled from deep in his chest as if he just remembered to breathe.

He handed rocks to Tim. "Put them at the edge of the shelf. We'll toss them into the water after we're done."

At first, the rocks were small and loosened easily. Then they got larger. Three large pieces fell next to Charlie, missing Tim's toes by inches. Then their sizes changed into small, flat sections. The opening, easy to pull apart at first, now resisted Charlie's efforts. It wasn't getting larger.

"What's the matter?" asked Tim.

"The rock's solid. I can't knock any more pieces out of it."

Tim knelt beside his friend. "No! We have to get outta here! We gotta get out!" He slapped and clawed at the wall with his bare hands. "He can't leave us here, Charlie. He can't leave us here! Tiny Bear laughed! I heard him. *We* heard him! He can't leave us here," he said with a defiant tone, his face hot.

"Don't you dare leave us here, Tiny Bear!" he shouted at the ceiling.

He picked a rock and along with his other hand, pounded at the wall. "Don't you dare! Don't you dare! You hear me?"

Charlie grabbed Tim's arms. "Stop. Calm down. He won't abandon us. Don't worry. He'll figure something out!"

Studying Charlie's features in the available light, Tim burst out laughing and crying.

"Calm down. You're scaring me. Tiny Bear will help. We'll be okay," said Charlie.

"I'm just happy to hear you say that. You don't think I'm crazy, because *you* believe in him too!"

"I sure do. I heard him laugh. I saw him, didn't I? Your poppa wouldn't lie. Besides, worry don't get you anywhere. It only makes you miserable. Tiny Bear won't give up on us. He'll help us."

Having given up knocking out more rock, Charlie crouched on the shelf and pulled at the blanket weighed down by the newly extracted rock. Pulling the blanket out from under the rock pile without ripping it would be impossible. After a pause, he said, "C'mon, we gotta push this pile over the edge."

At first, the boys sat behind the rock-pile, pushing with their feet. The pile budged an inch. Almost.

Charlie crouched behind the pile, placed a wad of blanket between his shoulder and the rocks, and pushed again. Nothing happened. Next, he placed one foot sideways in a wide crack of the shelf's floor for support. With all his strength, he pushed and grunted, determined not to give up. His face contorted from the force he demanded of his body. The pile slowly inched forward. Suddenly, it slipped over the edge, landing below in a great splash.

Charlie had nothing to hold on to. He yelled, "Tim! Grab my leg! Ti—!"

On cue, Tim immediately reached out with both hands, wildly grabbing to catch Charlie's leg, ankle, foot, *anything!*

Charlie and the rock-pile hit the water within seconds.

For Tim, reality suddenly became distorted.

It seemed like the splash boomed and echoed off the cave walls.

Did the water come from above, splashing all around him?

No, it splashed from below in giant, thunderous waves.

Tim became dizzy as the cave tipped and turned. Then it all stopped.

In shock from the sudden, unexpected event, Tim quickly crept to the edge.

Where was Charlie?

His eyes bulging, Tim strained to focus, searching the water's surface, yelling, "No-o-o! Charlie. Come back!"

The river swirled in ripples around the cave. So much water.

Minutes passed. Too many minutes. How long? How much time?

Under water, people can hold their breath for several minutes. But Charlie couldn't swim!

"Charlie, come back! Please, Tiny Bear! Charlie can't swim. Bring him back. Make him safe. Make it okay."

At that moment, Charlie emerged. His arms slapped the water as he sucked in air. He kicked his legs and swung his arms about, staying afloat.

"Charlie! You okay?" Tim yelled with relief.

"Blanket! The blank—" Charlie went under.

Tim understood what his friend had in mind. He immediately tossed the end of the blankets, anchored above, into the water. Clinging to the blanket's upper end, he expected Charlie to emerge once more to grab the lower end.

"Charlie! Grab the blanket. I got the blanket! Charlie! I did what you said!"

Through the blur of his teary eyes, Tim watched and waited.

"Charlie! I did what you said! I did what you said!"

Too much time had gone by. Tim shook his head. "No! Don't let him die! No! Tiny Bear! Get him back! Please!"

He burst into tears. Tears he had promised he would never shed flowed like the river outside.

He had promised himself to be grown up and in control. But this was way too much for Tim to handle.

He shivered, unable to control his grief. He tightened his grip on the blanket, howled, screamed, and growled, "Tiny Bear. Get him back! Get him back!"

Tim realized his screams wouldn't provide a solution for Charlie's problem, so he willed himself silent and watched the swirling water for signs of perhaps a hand coming up, and hopefully, for Charlie to suddenly bob up, gasping for air.

But Charlie didn't come up for air.

"Tiny Bear! You gotta help Charlie!"

Tim had to do something!

Through bleary eyes, he focused on the dark, swirling water, stood up and jumped in.

The second he entered the water, his left ankle and left rib cage hit a hard surface. Clutching his side for a split second, he grunted, letting bubbles escape through his lips. His eyes squeezed shut from the sharp pain. Determined to continue searching, he wished the pain away and groped for Charlie.

Underwater, Tim found it dark, cool, and filled with the churning, lapping sounds, along with his noisy escaping air bubbles. Each time he surfaced to breathe, he called out, "Charlie! Swim. Swim up. You need air! Charlie!"

Tim dove again and again, grabbing whatever he could to prevent the current from sucking him out of the cave and into the river.

After several attempts to find Charlie, Tim grew exhausted. His body felt limp, like a wet rag sloshing in a bucket.

His ankle throbbed, and his side shot a burning pain whenever he grabbed at the rock wall to anchor himself.

Charlie was nowhere. Tim shed tears not from physical pain, but for losing his friend.

The continued search for Charlie exhausted Tim. He didn't know which end of the cave Charlie body would be located. He had to stop and climb up to the shelf while he had some energy left to do so. He reached for the hemlock limb, hung on, and breathed hard, catching his breath. In the low light, he looked up to the shelf. It was high, but not as high as when they first climbed it. Could he climb alone? In the darkness? He had to.

Letting go of the limb, he swam to the wall where a now barely visible blanket hung. He pulled at it until it resisted. The blankets were still well anchored. Tim took a deep breath grabbed the blanket with both hands, and leaned back with his feet ready to walk up the wall. With each step, his hand grabbed farther up the blanket. His ribs shot near crippling pain at each pull. His ankle ached, and each step tortured it even more. After several slow upward pulls, he heard a tiny ripping noise. He stopped—it was only a slight rip.

"Please Tiny Bear, help me."

He took another step, another forward grab, and a pull, and another step, another forward grab, and a pull. He held his breath. Perhaps he'd make it after all.

The blanket gave way with a long ripping sound. Tim fell in a flash. His back slammed into the branches of the floating limb. The impact knocked the wind out of him. He had never experienced that before, but he knew that was what had happened. Part of him lay in the water, but enough of his body lay atop the web of branches to stop his descent. It had protected him from the rocks Charlie had shoved over the shelf and now sat piled beneath the water's surface.

Keeping still, he breathed deeply for several minutes. Paddling with his hands, he coaxed the limb toward the wall. There he placed his feet, anchoring himself. How could he climb without the blankets? And he was in a whole lot of pain.

Supported by a hemlock limb's splayed out branches, Tim was trapped in the flooded cave.

Charlie drowned.

That was not part of the plan.

And it was all Tim's fault.

Rescuing Charlie with an old blanket wouldn't have been a good idea after all. Since he weighed more, it would have ripped sooner. He would have fallen and hurt himself for sure on those rocks…or broken his back. But what happened was worse!

I tried. I tried to find him. Charlie drowned! It's all my fault.

Could Tim climb up again? He had to. And Tiny Bear? *He* sure wasn't around when needed.

"Tiny Bear! Where were you? Dad said you'd help if we needed you. We needed you. We still need you. Now!"

How could he climb again? Without help. Charlie's words came to him, "*…worry don't get you anywhere. It only makes you miserable.*" Tim sure was miserable. And he had to climb up again. Somehow.

With his feet, he pushed himself away from the wall. Paddling the floating limb with his hands, he grabbed at the rocky wall. One hand explored its surface until he found a bump—a protruding rock just under the surface of the water. His other hand discovered another bump higher up. Shifting his weight onto the first rock, he leaned toward the wall, pressing his cheek against its cool, hard surface.

He balanced himself on the toes of his good foot. The other foot's injured ankle begged for tenderness. All he could offer were a grimace and clenched teeth at every move. The darkness swallowed his surroundings. The river's noise grew distant as he focused on his climb. His very slow climb.

Each protruding rock and crevice offered hope. And a whole lot of pain. His body shook with the strain. Would he fall again? Could he continue? How many more steps? He needed more protruding rocks to grab and support him.

He found a crevice and more uneven rocks. His arms and knees trembled from the strain. He pawed farther out with his left hand, and pain from his rib cage shot out through that arm. He feared passing out.

"Breathe. Breathe."

He continued to explore. There it was, another rock. He grabbed it and pulled himself up. He investigated with his right foot and anchored his toes in a small fissure. This continued for what seemed like a very long time.

To Tim's surprise, he had reached the top!

But how could he let go of the wall? How could he jump onto the shelf? Not only did he hurt, he felt weak from the strain. And there was nothing to support him. No one to grab his belt and heave him up.

He had to raise both arms, but his left arm felt paralyzed. He was stuck. Both feet were raw, and his toes ached. How could he pull himself onto the shelf? Charlie wasn't there to help. He didn't want to fall again. He might not be lucky, having the branch beneath him a second time.

Pushing up with his toes to achieve a forward balance, Tim quickly swung his right arm up onto the shelf. There he hung on, afraid to move. How long could he remain in this uncomfortable and painful position?

He closed his eyes, pressed his chin on the shelf, and leaned his head slightly, touching his ear to the shelf floor.

"Tiny Bear. Please, please help. I believe in you. Dad wouldn't lie about you. You gotta be real. I need your help. Please!" he whispered.

For several minutes, he remained still. His breathing slowed, calming him.

Charlie's instructions came back to him. *"See yourself already on the shelf. Imagine you are that boy on the shelf. Be that boy on the shelf. You'll make it okay."*

He imagined himself as that boy safe on the shelf. He gingerly walked the fingers of his left hand up the wall, which slowly raised his left arm. His fingers reached the edge of the shelf. With a gradual, painful movement, he slid his hand forward, placing it beside the other. His lips twitched in his pain filled grimace.

Discovering a crack in the floor, he jammed all his fingers into it and pulled. His injured foot found another fissure in the wall. He planted his toes deep into the space and pushed himself upward.

He remembered Charlie's urging. *"Focus on the shelf. Go for it."*

Tim swung his good leg up and over onto the shelf. Pulling with his fingers; he quickly rolled himself away from the edge.

Lying on his back, he cried out, "Aah, aah!" The pain intensified. His stomach turned queasy, and a sour taste emerged from deep in his belly. He wanted to vomit.

He cried out, "Charlie!"

When he sat up, the vomit erupted onto his shirt. His echo dissolved into the distance. "No-o-o Charlie, no!" His voice quavered. "Charlie! Answer me! Come back! Charlie! Come back!"

Odors from the cave blended with his own sour smell as one. His wet clothing sucked the warmth from his body.

Tired and shivering, he wailed, "Charlie is my best friend. It ain't fair! First Dad. Now Charlie. He doesn't know how to swim. I couldn't help my very best friend! It ain't fair! It ain't fair!"

Infuriated by the echoes of his grief, he hollered, "Shut up, echo!" His face flushed and his throat raw, he moaned, "Tiny Bear! Why didn't you help? You're supposed to help people who believe in you!

"Why did you take Dad? And Charlie? I hate you! You hear me? I hate you! You can't let Charlie drown! Teach him how to swim! You hear me!"

Tim sat sobbing. Losing Charlie was more than he could stand. With his head in his hands, he felt powerless, distraught, and alone.

He was alone.

Chapter 28

I COME FOR YOU

Tim mumbled "Charlie" again and again as he drifted into semi-consciousness, unaware warmth and light had entered the cave. It arrived and sat beside him as he dozed.

"Ah, Awôsis. Ah, young child," whispered an echo from the cave walls.

Tim awoke. "Charlie?"

He was no longer chilled. What happened? He turned to his left. Someone sat next to him. An old man. Was he dreaming again? "Who-who are you?" asked Tim.

"I am Tsi'-dzis Awasos. You are Tim. I come for you."

Tim rubbed his eyes. When he reopened them, the old man had disappeared. The warmth lingered, and the light dimmed. Exhausted, unable to keep his eyes open, and clinging to the blanket supporting his aching ribs, Tim fell into a sound sleep.

He dreamed of Dad teaching him how to build a lean-to, how to swim, and, as a young child, being carried piggy-back style upstairs to his room at bedtime.

Deep in sleep, Tim didn't notice the gentle rocking motion of the canoe making its way upriver. Nor did he hear the ancient lullaby softly sung as a black hawk flew overhead.

Chapter 29

INSIDE THE WIGWAM

THE WIFE HELPED PULL the canoe ashore. The husband lifted Tim out of the canoe, carried him into the wigwam, placed him onto an awaiting mat, and covered him with a blanket.

Hours later, Tim half-awoke, turned over and peeked through his droopy lids, and spotted two people sitting by a fire.

This ain't the cave. And this ain't my blanket. How did I get here? Where am I? Am I still dreaming? That's it!

Dreams dropped him in strange places. Where was this dream going? Perhaps he'd see Salubrious Frog again. Why hadn't the frog helped him find Tiny Bear the last time?

The people at the fire looked like...Indians. Old Indians.

They're just ghosts. Don't move. They won't notice. Then I'll wake up from this dream in my bed, like always.

Tim often dreamt of ghosts at home in his bedroom, thanks to J. J. Jones.

Tim's remedy was to lay still with his head under the sheet; hold his breath, be sure no chest movement became visible to a passing ghost.

When he felt the ghost had gone, he released a slow exhale and shut his eyes. Then he'd fall asleep, secure in the thought that the ghost had gone elsewhere, to torment someone else. Hopefully, it was J. J. Jones!

But this time was different. His clothes were damp. He frowned. So, he *wasn't* home in his bed.

Wake up! Think this through.

The river. He had jumped into the river, trying to save Charlie. He hurt his foot and his rib cage. He climbed a rock wall in excruciating pain. But his foot didn't hurt anymore. Couldn't have been a bad injury. His ribs. The pain. Gone, too. What a relief! However, not totally convinced he was pain free, he twisted his foot and torso with sudden jerky moves.

It's true. No pain!

But he hadn't saved Charlie! He sucked in a shaky breath.

Being tired, he lay still with eyes closed. He wanted Dad and Charlie back. The bear, Tiny Bear, had let him down. He'd look for the bear again and tell it a thing or two. It wasn't fair, and that made Tim fume!

Did this couple know about Tiny Bear?

Tim's eyelids grew heavy. He fell asleep once more.

Next time he awoke, he surveyed his surroundings. Opposite him was a fire pit. Another person lay wrapped in a blanket opposite the fire pit. Tim stared. He focussed on the person's long hair. Dark and curly.

Roach? Is that...Roach? Sleeping there? Covered in what? Mud? Why is she here?

And that man? That's him! The old man from the cave, with a woman. His wife? Indians? Both of them. Roach ain't an Indian, but she's here with them.

This has to be a mixed up dream. Worse yet, with Roach in it, it has to be a nightmare!

Rolling onto his back, he examined the shelter. The framework resembled Dad's lean-to with bent, horizontal saplings tied to other straight, thicker, vertical saplings. The whole of it covered with tree bark.

A wigwam. Just like Charlie said. Charlie's smart about things like that. Tim paused at his thought. A tear welled in his eye. "It ain't fair!

First Dad, then Charlie. I want you back. Both of you!" he whispered and gulped, silencing a budding cry.

He turned to the couple and leaned on his elbows. They greeted him with a smile and a nod.

He didn't understand what had happened? Perhaps they had taken him out of the cave while he slept. Or he couldn't wake up from this baffling dream.

"Hello. How'd I get here? And Roach? How'd she get here?" said Tim.

The wife went to the fire, poured something into a clay bowl and brought it to Tim, saying, "Kzôbo, kadosmimek."

Frowning, Tim didn't understand. She motioned with her hands for him to drink. Tim sat up, nodded, and sipped the warm liquid. Soup! He was hungry. With a smile, he whispered, "Thank you, Ma'am."

After he finished his soup, he lay on his mat with eyes shut tight. He fought the sadness consuming his thoughts. *I'm dreaming, and I can't wake up. I don't want to dream anymore. I couldn't help my very best friend! Salubrious Frog, come back. Tell me where Tiny Bear is.*

Scanning the area, he noticed another person behind him with matted-down hair poking from the blanket. Could be a son or daughter. Why was that person wet? The hair curly. And dark. The couple seemed too old to have children. Perhaps a grandchild? But Tim never heard of Indians with curly hair like Roachelle's or Charlie's. Could-could it be...Charlie in that blanket? It couldn't be.

Turning to the couple, he sat up. "Is-is that Charlie?"

They nodded.

"Ah! I saw him go under. He drowned. No one can stay under water that long without drowning! That's not— I don't understand."

With a trembling hand, Tim reached over slowly and touched the blanket. It couldn't be a dream because he felt the blanket and Charlie's shoulder beneath it. Was this his body? Did they find him? And decided to bring him here? Were they going to bury him? They couldn't do that. He wouldn't let them. He had to bring Charlie's body home to Mrs. Wallace. He imagined Mrs. Wallace heartbroken. He remembered her grabbing Charlie's cheeks and kissing him on the forehead the previous morning. He was supposed to watch out for Tim. Now Tim was supposed to tell Mrs. Wallace that Charlie was...dead. All because of Tim's need to look for a bear.

Tim owed it to Charlie. He had to bring him home. But how could he bring Charlie home? He needed a plan. Uncle Sal, or perhaps the old couple could help. Before he spoke a word, a noise distracted him. Breathing? Snoring? Charlie?

Tim's heart raced. Charlie! He'd recognize that irritating snore anywhere! But he saw Charlie drown! How could this be? How did Charlie get here? Alive. How did Tim get here, too?

Tim was super okay with Charlie being alive. The relief Tim experienced dismissed his curiosity about how they both got there. Having Charlie snoring next to him was a miracle. With his hand covering his mouth, he smiled from ear to ear in disbelief, and a happy tear trickled down his cheek.

"If this is a dream. I don't want to wake up. I don't want to wake up in that cave without Charlie," he whispered.

Charlie stirred, rolled over, stretched his arms high, and yawned with a grunt. His eyelids flicked open. He stared at the ceiling for several seconds. Then, with a sudden motion, he turned his head toward Tim.

"How'd we get here?" said Charlie.

"Charlie. I think we're both caught in one of my mixed up dreams. I been expecting Salubrious Frog to drop in. Do you think we're dreamin'? Are-are you dead or alive?"

"Me? Dead or alive? Well, I see you and I see me. And we can't be having the same dream. Least I don't think so." He sat up, pulled at his shirt. "My clothes are damp. Oh yeah! I went for a swim. But...I can't swim." Charlie paused, then smiled. "Scared you, didn't I?" He poked Tim's knee.

Tim wanted to hug Charlie and communicate his joy at having him back among the living. Instead, he bumped his friend's shoulder with his fist and grinned. That covered all that needed saying, because he knew Charlie understood.

"How do you think we got here? This is unbelievable, ain't it?" whispered Tim. "I feel safe here with that couple. We're out of the cave and listen, the storm is over! I can't hear it."

"Couple?" Charlie turned toward the entrance. The Indian entered, followed by his wife. "They must have brought us here, or someone else did. They look like nice people. Hey! He looks familiar. What you suppose they're up to?"

"Dunno," said Tim.

The Indian sat by the fire and faced the boys. He glanced at and motioned his hand toward Roach.

"Is that who I think it is? Roach? Sleeping. All muddied up. How do you think she got here? Did you tell her she could come along?" whispered Charlie.

With a slight frown, Tim shrugged his shoulders high. "No. Why would I invite *her*? She's...a *girl*, and a *busybody*," said Tim, with his upper lip curled up.

Charlie stared at Roach. "She must'a followed us and got in trouble. Let's ask her when she wakes up."

The wife brought Charlie a bowl.

"It's soup. There's no spoon. You drink it," said Tim.

"Thank you, Ma'am," said Charlie with a nod and a smile. He eyed Roach and the couple as he sipped the soup. He'd just finished when Roach tossed the blanket aside and sat up. Her eyes searched the ceiling.

"Where's the hawk? What's going on?" said Roach.

"What hawk? And what are you doing here?" asked Charlie.

Roach pivoted open-mouthed, shocked to see the boys and the Indian couple seated at the fireside. She examined the dried mud covering her arms and clothing and surveyed her surroundings with a frown. Her focus returned to the couple. Her eyes narrowed.

"It's him. I *saw* him! The shadow-man in the storm, and this morning. The hawk was with him. Where's the hawk? Charlie, where—"

"What you talking about?" said Tim.

"Hello, Sir. Do you speak English?" asked Charlie.

The Indian nodded.

"You do? "Are you an Indian couple? I mean is she your wife?"

"Oho, yes. Siômo, my wife. I am Old Indian."

"I'm Charlie and my friend here is Tim, and this is Roach. We're all neighbors on Dodge Hill Road."

Old Indian nodded to the children, then to his wife, got up, and left the wigwam. The language was foreign, but he spoke English, too!

Charlie asked the wife. "What happened to us Siômo? Can you tell us how we all got here?"

Siômo shook her head. "N'ôkskuasis kazebaalmuk. Young girl wash. Kiuwô kazebaalmuk. You wash," said Siômo, pointing to the boys. And she followed her husband outside.

"Where do you think they came from?" said Tim.

"I don't know," said Charlie. "Looks like they live here. But where is 'here'?" They must have brought us to this place, and they're sheltering and feeding us. So, they're okay."

"Roach, you didn't tell us how you got here," said Charlie.

Her chin high, and her fingers picking the dried mud from her arm, she said with a defensive note, "How'd *you* get here yourself?"

"We don't know," said Tim. "We got trapped in a cave and couldn't get out 'cause it flooded. And now, we're here. With you."

After a pause, Roach replied, "I got lost in the storm. In the dark. A wolf tried to warn me, but I slid down a high muddy slope, anyway. I almost landed in the river. I would have drowned." She hesitated and looked to the ground. "I-I don't remember things very well. The hawk came in the morning, flying high, round, and round above that *man*! The shadow-man." Roach looked at the entrance and clutched her necklace. "Now I'm here! Why is this happening? Why me? I want to go home."

"There ain't no wolves in River Fork," said Charlie.

"I know what I heard! I heard them before at Gram's!"

"Hey! Okay. Maybe you did. It'll be fine. That's the important thing," said Charlie.

Tim chimed in. "Yeah. We'll be okay."

Looking at the boys through bleary eyes, Roach sucked in a shaky breath. She abruptly wiped her eyes, smearing the mud away in a slant. She now resembled a cat, a confused cat. The boys glanced to each other, not knowing what to say or do to calm her.

"Why are we all in this strange place? Are we prisoners?" said Roach.

Siômo returned and knelt at Roach's side. "Kiuwô kazebaalmuk. You wash." She stood, offered her hand to Roach and said, "Ponômuk. Come."

Noticing Roach's hesitation, Charlie said, "Don't worry. I don't think we're prisoners. We just need to wash up. She wants to help you clean up and maybe take care of all them scratches."

Siômo turned to Charlie and smiled.

With a faint grin aimed at Charlie, Roach glanced at the wife and stood up.

"It's okay. You'll be fine. She wants to help," Charlie repeated.

Roach's smile widened. This time she dared make eye contact with Charlie. Uncomfortable with her boldness, he looked away first.

Roach combed her fingers through her stiffened, muddied hair—her effort to look presentable. Siômo took Roach's other hand and guided her outside.

Curiosity overtook the boys. As one, they scrambled to the entryway. What was outside? Where was Roach being taken? Should they have let her go so easily; just like that? Without question?

Whispering, sharing their concerns, they watched Siômo pick a bundle from a large boulder before continuing on. Soon, both figures were beyond the embankment and out of sight.

At that moment, Old Indian emerged from the woods, heading back to the wigwam. The boys dashed back to their bedding.

Old Indian grinned as he stepped into the wigwam. Had he noticed the boys at the doorway? They sat where they'd been when he left, but their eyes betrayed their sense of guilt and mistrust.

Holding the entry flap for them to pass through, he said, "Ponômuk. Come."

The boys paused, like animals kept too long in a cage, suspicious of what might await them once set free.

Tim whispered, "Should we run for it?"

Charlie nudged him to follow and whispered back, "Not yet. We have Roach to think about. We can't run off and leave her."

"Nda sagzimek. No fear. Ponômuk. Come." He led them to the river, upstream from where Roach had gone.

Clothing similar to what the couple wore lay on the riverbank. Old Indian tugged at his sleeve, pointed to the river, and scrubbed his hands together. The boys understood. They pulled off their shirts, crouched, and dipped their hands into the cool water. They turned to thank their host, but he had vanished.

The boys washed themselves in the refreshing water without soap.

Examining the length and width of the calm river, Tim hoped to never experience a hurricane or a raging river again. Ever!

"Make sure you wash that smelly shirt real good, Tomata," said Charlie with a chuckle.

Tim sloshed his soiled clothes in the river. He welcomed the friendly tease of nicknames between friends. He would be Charlie's friend until they were as ancient as the old couple.

Chapter 30

CHARLIE EXPLAINS

THE BOYS SCRUBBED THEIR shirts and dungarees. Even though the Kool-Aid stain remained on Tim's shirt, they decided their clothes were clean enough, so they spread their laundry on a nearby bush to dry. Clad in their boxer shorts, they lay on a grassy patch to dry in the sunshine.

"The ground ain't soggy. Right after a flood? That ain't possible. Maybe we been here a bunch of days after the storm. That would explain why the ground is dry," said Tim.

"My clothes were damp when I woke up. Remember? So it can't be more'n a day," said Charlie.

"Yeah, I woke up with my shirt still wet and smelly from throw-up. You think it's tomorrow? I mean, the storm was *yesterday*. And this is *tomorrow* on the Saco River. Right?"

Charlie pondered Tim's questions. "It must be. Well, I *think* this is the Saco. But the river ain't running over the bank. Can't figure how all that water disappeared. Like magic! The cave—the whole place flooded. It takes a long time for that much water to disappear. Days. Weeks," said Charlie.

"Magic? You suppose Tiny Bear is doing all this? Or, could be, we all died. And we're in Heaven," said Tim. "If we're dead, then maybe I'll see Dad—"

"We didn't die! Tiny Bear did this. You said he'd help."

"Yeah, I did. But why this way? Why here? And what happened to you, Charlie? I mean, after you fell in the river, I saw you *drown!* That ain't no way to help us. You drowned! And now you're here. Alive." Tim frowned at the river. "I don't understand what I saw anymore."

Charlie scratched his head. "Drowned? Dunno. Maybe I did. Maybe not. Strange. Everything seemed to happen in slow-motion, while I moved as fast as I could at the same time. Understand? Strange. Very strange.

"When I fell, I thought, 'Grab something! Have Tim grab me—stop me from falling!' But I fell anyway. Right next to the rock pile that landed on top of the one we saw earlier. When I got to the bottom, I pushed myself up with my feet and kicked my way up.

"Poppa used to say, 'If you fall in the river, keep moving your arms and legs 'til someone comes for you. Keep moving.'

"I got scared, because no one knew we were in the cave, and I had to get us outta there! I moved my arms up and down, like jacking up a car, except I jacked myself up out of the water for air."

"You yelled for help. Remember? You said, 'The blanket!' I threw it over the side, but you disappeared," said Tim, muffling a cry inching its way up his throat.

"Yeah. The river dragged me under. I heard the current and air bubbles coming from my mouth. Holding my breath got near impossible, so I reached out all around for anything to climb on. I needed air. I knew my lungs would explode, and I'd drown if I didn't get air."

Tim stood, shook his head, paced back and forth with his hands flopping up and down. "I couldn't help you! I tried and tried. I'm sorry, Charlie. I—I wanted to get you outta that water and back on the shelf. So I jumped in! But the water was dark. I couldn't find you, no matter how many times I dove under. You disappeared. I'm sorry," Tim said in a whimper.

Charlie's eyes bulged in their sockets. "You jumped *in*? In fast moving water? To rescue me? You could have gotten dragged away!

I'm shocked. But I'm happy you made it back." Charlie sat up and poked Tim's leg. "You. Little Tomata Head. Jumped into the water to rescue *me?* It takes a *man* to do that. You ain't little anymore, no sirree. You may be short, but you ain't the little guy you used to be, Tomata."

"I got sick when I couldn't find you, I thought you drowned," said Tim, with lips quivering.

"Hey! Tiny Bear helped! I'm here now. He taught me how to swim."

Tim paused. "He did?"

"Yeah. He *did*. At first, the water was chilly. Then it got warmer. It felt like someone wrapped me in a warm blanket. Then I saw a light. Moving. In front of me. I thought, 'Follow that light. Betcha it's Tiny Bear.' I followed. For a while, it seemed my lungs would explode; then suddenly, they didn't bother me. Like in a dream. Everything dark. Strange. Magical. Then it grew lighter and lighter. I saw a big, dark thing in front of me. A tree trunk. In the water. I wrapped my arms and legs around it to stop moving and crawled up for air. Figured I'd stay glued to that tree.

"That's when I saw that hawk again. Remember? The one we saw at the campsite? It flew round and round. Then an old man—" Charlie snapped his head toward the camp. "*That's* who he is! I *knew* I seen him somewhere. Old Indian." Charlie pointed toward the wigwam. "He showed up in a canoe. And I wake up in his wigwam."

"Wait, I saw a bright light, then an old man—Old Indian—sat in the cave next to me. Then he disappeared, and I woke up in his wigwam, too," said Tim.

"How did he get in the cave? I was with you. No one else was there."

"He came after I tried to rescue you. He told me his name. Teezee Whatsis? Or something like that. He knew *my* name. Said he came for me. How'd he know where to find me?"

"Maybe you dreamed it," said Charlie.

"How could we both dream up the same Indian? And now I'm here with you and the Indian couple." Tim paused. "You really think Tiny Bear was in the water *with* you?"

Charlie nodded and smiled. "Yeah. He was there with me. Guiding me out of the cave. Up to that tree. He made me feel warm in the water.

That light? Yeah. He was there. Must 'a been with you too, cause you're here with me. Roach said she saw the 'shadow-man'—that Indian. And the hawk. Bet it's the same hawk we saw. You think they know about Tiny Bear?"

"I don't know," said Tim.

"Ask them."

"How would I ask? 'Oh, by the way, Sir, did you ever run into a tiny, laughing bear around here?' No, not 'run into.' That'd be deadly for the bear. How about, 'Did you ever see a tiny, laughing bear around here?' Sounds better." Tim shook his head. "Old Indian would probably laugh."

⁓ ✢ ⁓

Once dried off, the boys checked out their new clothes. Tim picked up a garment and frowned. "What are *these*?"

Charlie pressed a second, longer garment against his leg, checking the length. "They're called leggings. Covers your legs. Made from deerskin."

"How'd you know that? Wait! There ain't no pant part. You know, to cover your butt and stuff."

"Grampa's Abenaki friend wore leggings. I remember. I seen pictures, too. This skinny leather cord, at the top of the leggings, ties around your waist. Like a belt. So they won't fall down."

Tim nearly peed himself from laughing so hard. "That won't matter, because nothing's covered up to start with! At least *we* have underwear."

Charlie waited with a smirk, which Tim read as, "Settle down. That ain't polite."

Tim stopped laughing, but his giggles were at the ready behind his tightly pressed lips.

"And you wear this long narrow piece of cloth like a diaper." Charlie gave Tim a Cheshire Cat grin.

"Diaper? I ain't wearing no diaper. I ain't no baby!" Tim's giggles evaporated.

"The same belt holds the cloth in place. Because it's long, you slip the cloth up behind the belt and hang the ends over the belt, in front and on your backside. Like an all-in-one diaper and skirt."

Dumbfounded, Tim stared as Charlie donned the leggings, belt, and the all-in-one diaper and skirt.

"That looks silly. I ain't wearing no skirt. In front of the Indian? And his wife? And Roach?"

"Why not? It's polite to wear what they offer us."

"Well. It's-it's too hard to figure out. Besides, you look silly with your bony hips and your underwear sticking out like that."

"You don't like my hips? Don't worry, the shirt covers 'em. See?" He let the shirt slip down into place. "Just right. Out of sight." Charlie held back a giggle.

"Oh, I don't know. I ain't no Indian. Besides, look at *my* shirt. It's too *big*. Looks like a nightgown. *Women* wear nightgowns. How 'bout we wear our own clothes?" Tim's voice cracked and squeaked.

Finally, the boys agreed the old couple looked fine in their clothing. But even for Charlie, the clothes were uncomfortable, so very different from theirs. Compared to cotton, leather proved a tad rough on the skin.

The boys compromised. They returned to camp wearing damp dungarees and their new deerskin shirts. Tim included his own belt to shorten the shirt by pulling it up and out over his belt. He didn't mind the bulge created at his waist; at least it didn't look like a nightgown.

Chapter 31

ANGRY AT GREAT SPIRIT

OLD INDIAN SAT AT the fire with eyes closed. The boys sat nearby, waiting. Tim examined the old man's wrinkled yet handsome face. To him, it personified strength and kindness.

"I wonder if he's a chief. Maybe a warrior," Tim whispered into Charlie's ear.

Charlie leaned over, cupping his hand over his mouth. "I think all male Indians *were* warriors."

"Kiuwô, mannanékkañn. You be lost boys," said Old Indian.

"I don't think so," said Charlie. "We went to a cave, and it flooded and trapped us. We know how to get home. Just got trapped. Trapped in a cave is all. Not lost."

"You be lost boys."

Charlie frowned for a moment, then asked, "What do you mean, 'lost'?"

"K'mitongwes. Your fathers. Gone. No fathers. You be lost boys."

Tim and Charlie exchanged surprised glances.

At that moment, Siômo and Roach returned.

Roach brushed her clean, wet hair with her fingers, pulling it over her shoulders. She was barefoot and wore a plain deerskin dress.

With her damp hair draped over her shoulders and dark complexion, Tim imagined that's what an Indian girl probably looked like long ago.

The only difference—the curly hair and that red necklace. Why did she wear that necklace? Every day?

And her scratches—all gone! Just like me. I woke up in the wigwam with my injuries and pain gone!

Siômo motioned at Roach to sit with the boys. Roach peeked at Charlie, hesitated, then stepped over and sat close to him, her elbow touching his.

His personal space invaded, Charlie placed his hands flat at his sides, picked himself up slightly, and moved about six inches away. Frowning, he turned to Tim, gave a slight head nod toward Roach, and rolled his eyes, as if asking, "What's with her?" Tim responded with a quick "Heck if I know" grimace, with his lips in a crooked, silly grin.

Siômo offered a bowl to Roach. "Thank you Ma'am. My last meal was two of Gram's biscuits and wild berries from the woods yesterday morning."

While Roach sipped her soup, Old Indian spoke. "Nda sagzimek. No fear, majekisgad kwelbiwi. Bad weather behind. Thank Kchi Niwaskw, Great Spirit, for sun today, tomorrow, and for many days after. Thank Great Spirit for your fathers. For many days after your fathers. Your fathers come to you today, tomorrow. They be with you. I see. Your fathers be with you."

Old Indian, his chin firm, his head held high, gazed beyond his guests.

To satisfy his growing curiosity, Tim glanced over his shoulder. Would he see Dad behind him? Charlie nudged his leg—a warning to listen.

Old Indian smiled at Roach. "Nokmes. Grandmother. Old. Tired. You help grandmother. She weep many days. No daughter. You weep many days. Nda Kigawes. No mother."

With her bowl halfway to her lips, Roach blinked at Old Indian. She turned, looked to Siômo, to Charlie, and back to Old Indian. Placing the bowl down, her hands drifted up to find her necklace.

"Mom will come back. She promised to come back. To get me." Her voice faded as she twirled a red crystal bead. "She promised. Mom promised."

"Mother. Gone. You help Grandmother. Grandmother tired. Mother not come today, not come many days. You help Grandmother."

Roach stroked her necklace, and a tear trickled onto her new dress.

Tim stared. *Why isn't Roach angry? If her mother is alive, why isn't she in River Fork? It ain't fair to Roach. Like it ain't fair for Dad to be gone. Parents are supposed to be* home *with family!*

Old Indian turned to Tim. "K'mitôgwes, nidoba agema. Your father, my friend. I be with him. He be with you."

Tim took a quick breath. "Your friend? You know Dad?"

"Good man. Great Spirit be with your father. Your father spirit be with you."

Tim stood up, gathering his thoughts. "*I* want *more* than his *spirit.* I want *all* of Dad back. If he was such a 'good man,' then why did he *die?* Why didn't Great Spirit leave Dad with *me!* With *Mom!*"

He dropped to his knees near the fire pit and stared at the soil. He didn't want to hear about spirit stuff. He wanted Dad in the flesh. Keeping his head down and clawing at the soil, his ears grew warm and his face flushed.

"Do *you* know Tiny Bear? Dad *believed* in him. *I* believed in him. Why didn't he help Dad again, like he did when Dad was a boy?"

Old Indian raised his arms with palms up, eyes closed. "It is great decision for man, woman, child to die. Great Spirit decide when you are born, when you walk the land. Great Spirit decide when you die, when you leave the land. It is great decision."

Tim leaned forward, his elbows resting on the dusty soil, his hands digging at the ground, his head low. "But that was *Dad!*" he growled into the soil. His breath stirred the tiniest particles of ash and bits of leaves.

Old Indian lowered his head and listened.

"It's not right. Tiny Bear and Great Spirit can bring him back. I want him *back*. He left me and Mom alone. *We* want him back."

Roach, with eyes glistening and her mouth open, stared at Tim. Charlie said nothing. Old Indian waited. All remained silent.

Tim's mind raged on. *I will not cry. Not anymore! I'm not a baby. I'm almost thirteen.*

He sat back on his heels unable to continue, for he slowly realized he had indeed been furious about Dad's death. Was Salubrious Frog right? The frog's words filled his head:

"...You are very angry with someone. That is why you wish to speak with Tiny Bear. Am I correct, Sir?"

Tim shook his head. His voice firm, he said, "It still ain't fair even if it's Great Spirit who took Dad." He pointed at his friend. "It ain't fair for Charlie either. Or-or for Roach."

No one spoke.

"Charlie? Roach? Say something."

Charlie shook his head. "What you want us to say? There ain't anything you can do 'bout it. You can't get them back. I know how you feel. Roach probably knows how you feel."

Roach nodded slowly at Charlie, then at Tim.

Tim's throat tightened like a knot. "I—" His voice squeaked and croaked. He couldn't speak. In frustration, he stood up once more, slamming the fistfuls of ash and soil he had dug up around him into the fire. The flames rose high for a few seconds. Sparks twirled higher, and in an instant, fell around Old Indian, extinguishing themselves before touching the ground. Old Indian never flinched.

Breathing deeply, with his head tilted back, Tim closed his eyes. *Sure, Charlie accepted it. And Roach? Where's her mom? I'd be super angry if Dad was alive, decided to just drive away one day and didn't come back.*

With a hoarse voice, he said, "You-you say you know Dad? I don't know *you*. And Tiny Bear? He was Dad's friend! Dad said so! He met him once. Tiny Bear rescued Dad and Uncle Sal when they were kids.

"Why didn't he save Dad this second time? He was his friend! Remember? It ain't fair!" Tim dropped to his knees and sat back on his heels.

"I'm angry at Tiny Bear. And, yeah, maybe at Dad. He convinced me Tiny Bear would help anytime I needed him.

"If Tiny Bear likes to help, why won't he just let Dad come back? He let Charlie come back. Where's Dad now? You think maybe Dad doesn't want to come back? Is that it? If he doesn't want to come back, then yeah, I'm really *super* angry at him."

"Calm down, Tim. It's not your poppa's fault. It's no good to be angry at him because he's gone. You got yourself all worked up. Why do you yell at the people who rescued us? Just because you can't get what you want?" asked Charlie.

"Well, then I'm angry at Great Spirit. He took Dad and he won't bring him back." With a glare, he pointed at Charlie. "You came back."

"But I didn't *die*. You can't be angry at Great Spirit. That would be like being angry at...God." Charlie reached out, offering his hand.

"Great Spirit ain't the same as God!" Tim shouted, jumping to his feet, stepping away from Charlie's reach.

"Great Spirit be Creator. Your God be Creator. Great Spirit be God. There be many names for God—for Great Spirit," said Old Indian.

With a pleading expression, Tim looked from the couple to Charlie. His arguments were useless. Nothing he said would make things any different. He wanted to run out and scream at the sky, the trees, the birds. That black hawk. He wanted to find it, grab it by its neck, shake it, and hurt it.

At that thought, his knees trembled and his lower lip quivered; he breathed deep. Plopping down onto the soil, he sat cross-legged. He lowered his chin to his chest and stared at the fire. Thoughts filled his head.

Just like a little kid. I just had a tantrum. I'm not a little kid. My head hurts. I'm out of control. Stop this!

He peeked at Old Indian. Why did he yell at him? And why did he throw dirt into the fire? He could have hurt him with sparks flying all around.

A brat. I acted like a brat.

After an uncomfortable silence, Tim wondered if Charlie was right.

That couldn't really be him thinking of doing bad things to get Dad back. He considered himself a good person, like Dad, Mom, and his grandparents.

Anger made him want to do bad things. Hurt people and that hawk. He had to stop being angry because he couldn't have his way. It wasn't fair for him and Mom to lose Dad. But what he did just now wasn't right or fair either.

Straightening his posture, Tim met Old Indian eye to eye. "I-I'm sorry, Sir. I don't want to be angry at you or Great Spirit or Dad. I just want Dad back. All of him. For me. For Mom."

"Father, be with you. He be proud," said Old Indian.

"Dad? Proud? What do you mean?"

"You are good person. Like Father.

"Life is like River. Great Spirit give River. River flow in peace. It give food, water, travel. One day River be angry. It take back all it give. Soon River flow in peace again.

"Life, like River, give peace. One day Life be angry. It take away all we love. Then *we* be angry.

"But we be one with Life, again. Great Spirit give Life, give peace. You be like River. You find peace. Speak to Father. He be with you now and for many days. He help find peace."

Watery eyes blurred Tim's vision. "Dad is with me? He'll always be with me?"

Old Indian nodded. After a brief silence, he got up, walked to Tim, gently placed a hand on his head, "You eat. Sleep. Soon, I bring you home." He left the wigwam. Siômo lifted the entry flap, secured it open, and followed her husband.

Relieved from the stress of the encounter, the three friends inhaled the fresh air entering the wigwam. They had a lot to think over.

Roach touched Charlie's shoulder. "Who's Tiny Bear?"

"Oh. Uh, I'll tell you when we get home," said Charlie.

"You promise?" Roach's eye twinkled as she gave Charlie a broad smile.

"Yeah. I promise." He stood aside, letting Roach step out before him. Avoiding her smile, he looked to his friend. "You coming, Tim?"

"Coming. Yeah, I'll be there in a minute," said Tim. He needed a moment to think about Dad, Mom, and now, the prospect of getting home again. He had seen the bear. It was real. Would he see it again? From what he knew about the bear so far, it didn't speak. But that was silly. Bears don't speak. So how did it become Dad's friend? How would Dad *know* it was his friend?

Old Indian said Dad's spirit was with Tim. Yet Tim wanted more than Dad's spirit nearby. Therefore, he clung to the belief that Tiny Bear's magical powers could help bring Dad back.

I'm going to find *that bear!*

Meanwhile, how would he even know Dad's spirit was with him? He needed proof.

"Give me a sign, Dad. Let me know you're *really* with me," he whispered.

As he turned to follow Charlie and the others out of the wigwam, his pant leg fluttered against his calf, but he was inside a wigwam and there was no breeze. Something whisked by him, touching his left shoulder. He felt goosebumps on his arms. What happened? He turned back to see.

There, in front of him, stood a forest. And ahead, the black hawk, flying into it. All this inside the wigwam? How could that be?

Tim turned to face the entryway. It wasn't there. "What happened? Where's everybody?" He groaned. "Am I in another mixed up dream? Is this where Salubrious Frog pops in again? I want to wake up! *Please!*"

In the distance, the hawk perched on a branch along a path that led into the forest. Tim followed the path.

The forest sounds mingled with an erratic buzz, a sound Tim recognized—a chainsaw.

Had to be a logger. Perhaps the logger could help them get home. Tim ran, shouting, "Hello! Hello? Can you hear me?"

The buzz continued. The saw made familiar sounds, its small engine coughing, choking, sputtering, and egging the user to rev it up, to keep it running.

Tim arrived below the treed hawk. It bobbed its head and stared at the clearing ahead. Following its gaze, Tim saw a logger cutting a tree. The saw continued to sputter, then suddenly stalled. The logger pulled the starter recoil cord with his right hand to restart the saw. With each pull, the saw, while in his left hand, snapped upward and wobbled briefly in midair. Tim knew that was a dangerous way to restart a chainsaw. Dad had said so many times, but he said lots of loggers do it anyway when they're tired. With the third pull, the chainsaw wobbled wildly; the blade struck a nearby tree trunk, jumped back, and hit the logger in the shoulder. The impact knocked the logger to the ground.

Stunned at what he witnessed, Tim bolted. But he could barely move! What was wrong with him? And he needed help to pull the logger out of the woods. "Charlie! Help! An accident. Come now!" he shouted.

No one answered.

He continued to run, but the distance between him and the logger seemed to grow wider. What was happening? This was insane. The man needed help, and Tim couldn't reach him.

At last! Someone stepped from the woods into the clearing.

"He needs help! He had an accident. Help him!"

The newcomer, apparently unaware of what had happened, set his tools at the edge of the clearing, removed his hat, wiped his brow, and sat under a tree.

"Mister! That logger is hurt! Help him!"

Tim's feet grew heavy, as if anchored in concrete. He craned his neck, keeping watch over the downed lumberman. There he was on the ground, bleeding, and the other logger didn't seem to know.

"Help him! Tiny Bear! Help that man."

Just then, Tim heard a muffled cry for help. The other man heard it too. He bolted up and ran while unbuttoning and pulling off his own shirt. Once he reached the downed logger, he knelt at his side and wrapped the shirt around the bloody shoulder. That done, he scooped up the logger and ran into the woods beyond.

Tim was relieved. The logger would get help.

Suddenly, something black as coal soared in the air, up and down, like an angry ocean wave aimed at Tim. Inches from his face, he recognized the black hawk. Its eyes locked with his. Avoiding collision by a breath, the bird swooped up, and disappeared.

Tim looked to the forest. It had vanished, too. His feet were no longer sluggish. With his heart pounding, he turned and approached the wigwam's entryway. What had he just witnessed? Why had he seen that logger? Then the hawk, trying to communicate something. What was it telling him?

Something touched his shoulder again. He pivoted. "Charlie?"

No one was there. Sensing a presence, he peered intently through the shadows of the wigwam. There from the fire pit, a misty silhouette—a human form, barely outlined by the dying embers, emerged and quickly vanished.

"Tim, I love you. I will always be with you." There had been no sound, but he heard it in his head.

"Dad?" His pant leg at his calf stirred. "Dad!"

He remembered the breeze at the cemetery. He wiped the sudden tears that blurred his vision. "You were in the cemetery with me, weren't you? And here, now."

He stepped to where the silhouette had appeared, but there was nothing there.

"Dad?" Tim stared at the dying embers.

It's you! Dad! You talked to me.

Tim couldn't wait to share his latest experience with Charlie. But then, Charlie'd probably say he was dreaming again.

Perhaps he could speak with Old Indian. Privately. No, he couldn't leave his best friend out.

His big problem was Roach. He didn't want her around when he talked to Charlie. She was a busybody and asked too many questions.

Chapter 32

A FINE CANOE

Curious about the strange clothing she found folded and stored in the wigwam, Roach asked Charlie to explain what they were. He turned, winked at Tim, and explained without mentioning the words "diaper" or "skirt."

Thinking about what Charlie said, Roach picked up the long, narrow cloth. "Oh, I see. Just like a skirt."

Charlie smiled.

"Not a skirt, silly. A covering for front and back," said Tim, his ears warming.

Roach paused. "Oh. You mean it hides your behind and...stuff. Like a diaper?" said Roach, grinning at Tim.

Tim's ears and cheeks burned.

Roach giggled and shook her head. "You need a talk about the birds and the bees." She walked away.

Frowning, Tim shook his head. "She talks about my 'stuff,' then says I need a talk about birds and bees. Why'd she say that?"

"She's talking about sex," said Charlie.

"You said 'puberty' was about sex."

"Yeah. But talking about 'the birds and the bees' is *code* for talking about sex. She teased you because she saw how embarrassed you were about the diaper. She probably doesn't know a whole lot more than you about the birds and the bees."

"I'm gonna be thirteen. You gotta tell me more. So I don't sound stupid like I just did."

"You'll find out. And you're not 'stupid', you're just ignorant."

Tim stared at Charlie. "That sounds just as bad. What's the difference?"

"If you're ignorant, that means you haven't learned something yet. You just don't know until you educate yourself.

"But if you're stupid, that means you don't have the intelligence or ability to learn or understand. Like walking into a wall and doing it over and over, wondering why the wall is there. That's kind of exaggerated, but you understand what I'm saying?"

"Okay, yeah. I got it. So, when? When can I learn about the birds and the bees so I don't sound ignorant and embarrass myself like I just did?"

"Talk to your momma, 'cause I ain't gonna tell you."

"Why do you tell me little bits, then suddenly it's all a big secret? If it's a secret, Mom probably never heard about it."

Charlie smiled and shook his head. "Oh, she knows. You gotta ask. She'll tell you."

"Maybe Mom and Uncle Sal talk about puberty when they're alone, then change the subject when I walk in."

Charlie burst out laughing and shook his head. "No. I don't expect so. Ask your momma about all of it—puberty; the birds and the bees."

Later, the three friends explored the river's edge beyond the campsite.

"I figure we're in the Lower Wood. But where?" said Tim.

"We've explored the Lower Wood for years and we pretty much know the trees, rocks, and trails. I don't recognize any of the rocks near the river. And these trees. They're the darnedest biggest, trees I ever seen. Never seen so many big ones," said Charlie.

"Why does it matter what part of the woods we're in? We're not wet, we have food. I'm not afraid to be here. We can come back to visit that old couple sometime. Bring them one of Gram's pies. *You'd* like her pies." Roach directed her smile at Charlie.

"*I* like her pies," said Tim.

Let's go find your cave," said Roach.

Charlie frowned. "Hold on. Didn't we just say we don't recognize the area? And I'm sure it ain't around here."

"Well, if you don't look, you'll never see." Roach hurried past the boys, carefully picking her way with her bare feet, heading downstream along the riverbank.

As if on cue, both boys shook their heads.

Without further discussion, and careful not to step on stones or broken twigs, they trailed behind her. After half an hour of walking, Charlie announced he was going back and turned around. Tim followed.

Roach eventually returned to the campsite to find the boys. "If we followed the river another mile or two farther downstream, we could've found the cave."

Charlie scowled, plunged his hands deep into his pockets, and tilted his head. "It could be *upstream*."

"After we go home, we'll go back to the river and find the cave for sure. Then we'll visit their campsite again. I'll bring a baker's dozen of Gram's biscuits for the couple. A baker's dozen—that's thirteen."

"We know what a 'baker's dozen' is," said Charlie with a sneer.

"Yeah. That's a figure of speech for twelve plus one. What happened to the pie?" asked Tim.

With eyes closed, her lips pressed tight, Roach turned, raised her chin. "I'll bring that too!"

"Apple?"

She crossed her eyes, shaking her head. "Okay! Apple." She turned from Tim to Charlie and smiled. "Well? That sound good to you?"

Charlie stared at Roach for a few seconds, shook his head, and walked away. Tim followed.

Old Indian called out and motioned the boys to come. Arriving at a grove of trees along the shore, Tim paused and inhaled the combined aroma of pine, spruce, and hemlock. The forest scent reminded him of the Old Wood near his home, and the Lower Wood at the river.

"Gee. These trees are gigantic like the others!"

Ahead, at the river's edge, a birch-bark canoe sat propped upside down on two logs near another fire pit where coals glowed hot beneath a wooden grill.

From a cut made in a spruce tree with his stone ax, which now lay at the base of the tree, Old Indian collected the pitch into a bowl made of birch-bark.

Charlie asked, "Can we help?"

"Oho. Yes, Nia agukimômuk. I teach." Old Indian handed Charlie the bowl filled with gobs of sticky pitch.

Peeking into the container, Tim's eyebrows arched high up his forehead. "We supposed to eat that?"

Old Indian chuckled. "Bring to fire."

The heat soon softened the pitch. He added animal fat drawn from a clay pot and stirred the combination with a stick. Next he sprinkled powdered wood ash scooped from beneath the burning embers of the fire pit, and with his stick, stirred the mixture until it darkened. Once it turned black, he dipped a piece of birch bark into it, checking its thickness and tackiness.

"For canoe. Water not come in."

"Yeah, pitch'll make the canoe seams watertight," said Charlie.

"You know about canoes, too?" said Tim.

"Yup. When I was six, I wanted to surprise Grampa. Seeing lots of black stuff on his canoe, I scratched most of it off, to clean it up. I hoped he'd notice the great job I'd done. Well, as soon as we stepped in and pushed away from shore, he sure noticed. It sank."

"Did you know it was *your* fault?"

"Yeah, it took a split second to know I was in *big* trouble. He sent me home drenched and crying. The next day he brought me back and taught me how to seal the seams with black pitch. After it dried, we went fishing."

Charlie chuckled along with Tim. Old Indian shook his head and smiled.

Tim wondered how long it would take the three of them to seal the canoe. "How big is the canoe?" he asked.

When Charlie spread his hand wide from forefinger to thumb, it measured about six inches. So, he counted hand widths from one end of the canoe to the other. "Twenty measures. The canoe is about ten feet long," he said.

Dropping to his knees, he peered underneath. "It's got wooden slats and ribs. Room for more'n three grown-ups to sit and paddle. Ain't it a beauty? It's the darnedest, biggest, nicest looking canoe I ever seen."

"It sure is fine. And big," said Tim.

Before working with the pitch, the boys set their shirts aside.

Unaccustomed and clumsy at the task, Tim got pitch on his hands, elbows, neck, face, and hair. Scratching and tugging at the black, sticky blotches created more blotches. Noticing Tim's problem, the Indian dipped his fingers into the animal fat. "Kazebaalmuk. Wash." He taught Tim how to scrub with the fat. Tim stuck his fingers into the fat and rubbed it into the blotches.

"It worked, it unstuck me!"

Charlie picked up an oar, admired it, then made paddling motions. "Gosh, I sure would like to paddle this canoe upriver."

"And you can teach *me* how to paddle. We could paddle home. Whatever direction *that* is."

Charlie nodded and continued paddling, navigating up the Saco River in his imaginary canoe.

Chapter 33

MAKING MOCCASINS

WHILE THE BOYS HELPED Old Indian, Roach made her way to the large cooking fire pit outside the wigwam. A circle of large stones outlined its edges. A huge clay pot rested on thick logs over the pit.

The pot held a mystery stew that simmered and produced a pleasant aroma. Roach searched for a spoon to stir the mixture like Gram usually did. Siômo gave Roach a small bowl, encouraging her to dip it in for a taste.

"Yum! It's so good. All you need is a little salt and pepper."

Siômo smiled and turned. "Ponômuk. Come."

Roach followed her into the wigwam. Siômo unrolled a piece of tanned leather on the wigwam's dirt floor. She smoothed the leather flat with her palms, fetched two charred sticks from the interior fire pit, and handed one to Roach. "You make mkezen+al. Moccasin. Nia agukimômuk. I teach."

"Me? I make a mess just stuffing feather pillows," said Roach with a whine. "Besides, I *have* shoes." She looked down. "*Had* shoes...muddy shoes."

Siômo placed two cut leather patterns onto the rolled out leather and pointed to Roach. "Make moccasin for you. For boys."

Roach ran her hand over the hide, feeling its tough, sturdy texture. "What kind of leather is this?"

"Great Spirit give deer." Siômo traced her charred stick along one template. She nudged Roach's elbow. "You make."

As Roach traced, the template slipped. Siômo demonstrated how to keep the template in place with one hand while tracing with the other. Once Roach finished tracing, she peeked at the Siômo's moccasins decorated with colored beads. "Will my moccasins look pretty like yours?"

"Oho. Yes. Pretty."

The next tool was a curved stone with a sharp edge.

"Cut moccasin." Siômo motioned along the edge of the drawn pattern. Roach's first attempt didn't make a dent in the leather. She returned the stone to Siômo, and watched her grip the stone, push down and cut through a short segment of leather. Siômo handed the tool back to Roach. This time, Roach pressed the cutting stone down hard and carefully cut along the pattern lines she had drawn on the leather.

She held up her first cut-out, making its "wings" flap up and down in the air. "I made a giant butterfly!"

Next, from a rabbit pelt with fur still attached, Siômo cut a piece shaped like the sole of a foot, placing it in the middle of Roach's "butterfly."

"That protects your feet when you walk, and it feels so soft!" said Roach.

"Oho. Yes."

Roach picked up the cutting stone and frowned. "It would be easier to cut with scissors. Gram has scissors and a sewing machine. You ever use a sewing machine— Oh, guess not. If you had electricity, you wouldn't need a fire pit to see inside your wigwam. Anyway, scissors make cutting easier. You could buy a pair. You go to River Fork's Five and Dime to buy things, don't you?"

Siômo sat back on her heels, smiling. "N'ôkskuasis idôzik kassi. Young girl talk much. Taôlawi ahamo+ak. Like chicken." She giggled and handed over a white needle with a large eyelet.

"We have chickens. Maybe I like them because they talk a lot. Maybe *they* like *me*, because *I* 'talk much, like chicken.'"

They both giggled.

Roach examined the needle. "Chicken bone? It's pretty strong for a chicken bone. Did you make this?"

"Oho. Yes. I make. Not chicken. Deer."

Once assembled, Roach added a leather cord to tie the moccasin snug to the foot. Siômo took two pouches from a nearby larger birch-bark tray and placed part of the contents into a small clay dish.

"What is that?"

"Porcupine quill. Moose hair. Make moccasin be pretty."

Once completed, Roach examined the moccasins. "They look nice with quills and moose hair stitched in. Gram loves to sew. She would like these."

Roach lifted one pair, showing them off. "I made little quill decorations around the moose hair on these especially for Charlie. I hope he likes them." She stroked the soft rabbit fur lining. "His feet will be snug and happy in these."

"Happy? People happy. Feet not happy. Feet warm, not hurt," said Siômo.

"We say 'happy' because they feel good. Warm feels good. Okay, not happy feet. Warm feet. Thank you for helping me make these, Siômo.

"*Siômo*. I like your name. But Gram says I should call grownup ladies Mrs., or Ma'am. Is that okay?"

"Oho. Yes. Okay."

That afternoon, the boys returned to the wigwam. Smudges remained on Tim's forehead and hair. "Ma'am, do you have soap, so's I can wash?"

"Soap? Nda. No. No soap. Ponômuk. Come." The wife cleaned off the remaining pitch with more fat and warmed water. Tim grimaced while she scrubbed and rubbed the tar from his hair and face.

"Hey, it worked. You look nice and *red!* Same color as your hair!" said Charlie.

Tim grinned. "Thank you, Ma'am."

Siômo nodded.

Later that day, everyone gathered to sit at the interior fire pit. Siômo handed a deerskin bundle to Roach.

Roach stood up, facing everyone. She pointed down to her new moccasins. Her cheeks flushed. "I made these today."

"They look nice," said Charlie. Tim nodded in agreement.

She placed the bundle on the ground, reached inside it, and pulled out a pair of moccasins. "These are for you, Charlie. Made special, *just* for you."

Charlie hesitated, then mumbled, "Gosh, Roach, I—"

Ignoring Tim who cupped his hand over his mouth, hiding a grin, Charley sat there with a frown.

Roach's cheeks warmed. "Just take them!"

Charlie jumped up, took the moccasins, turned them over, and patted the fur lining.

"They'll make your feet happy. And warm." Roach took his hand and moccasin within her left hand, and traced the decoration at the edge with her right forefinger. She nodded toward Siômo and said, "Mrs. Siômo showed me how to make this design with porcupine quills and moose hair. Do you like it?"

"Gee, Roach. You made these? Gosh! They're fine looking. Thank you. I-I have nothing for you. We made black pitch. Don't think you'd like that much." Charlie's face flushed with a pink glow as he pulled his trapped hand and moccasin from Roach's hold.

Tim noticed Charlie's face change to a rosy color. *I'll be— Charlie's blushing!*

"Oh, that's okay. I made a pair for Tim, too." Roach pulled out a second pair and handed them to Tim.

Tim stood and accepted his gift. "I don't either. I mean, I don't have a present for you. But these look mighty fine, Roach. Thank you." To his relief, they weren't "made special" just for him. He held them up for all to see. They were plain, and he smiled wide at Charlie who sat down with a grunt and a frown.

By evening, the canoe was watertight, and the three guests sported new, warm moccasins with happy feet inside.

Because Roach was constantly nearby, or they were busy with chores, Tim hadn't talked to Charlie or the Indian about his experience in the wigwam.

Why had he seen that awful accident in the woods? And Dad's silhouette in the fire pit? He needed to speak with Charlie. Soon.

Chapter 34

ALWAYS WITH YOU

A NEW MORNING PEEKED in the eastern sky as Tim stepped out from the wigwam to digest all the events of his failed camp-out. Charlie had suggested Dad probably talked to Tim through Salubrious Frog. Or perhaps in his dream Uncle Sal was Salubrious Frog. Maybe Tim wanted his uncle's help. Uncle Sal stopped him from reaching Dad when the ambulance hauled Dad away a year ago. Tim had talked little with Uncle Sal after that. They didn't like each other. Was he angry at Uncle Sal? Why would Uncle Sal help now? Why would he appear as a frog? With a beard? Uncle Sal didn't even have a beard. The more Tim thought about what had happened, the more he didn't understand.

He shook his head and spoke quietly to avoid waking the others. "Dad, wherever you are, stay with me and Mom. You know my birthday is coming up. I'll be thirteen! Wish you were here. Not just your spirit, but all of you. For real!"

Old Indian said Dad would always be near, and that pleased Tim. But he hadn't believed it until he witnessed Dad in the fire pit. Why a fire pit? Did that mean he didn't go to Heaven? Tim definitely needed to talk to Charlie. Alone. Without Roach snooping around.

When did Old Indian become Dad's friend? Dad never mentioned an Indian friend. Ever.

"It's been a year since you died. And Old Indian said, I been lost since then. He's right, 'cause I still want you back. I just know Tiny Bear is near here. I wanted to find him *before* we went back home 'cause I wanted him to use his magic and bring you back.

But we been gone too long. We *gotta* get home soon. Mom, Mrs. Wallace, and Gram must be worried about us."

The sun rose above the horizon, and Tim stepped back into the wigwam.

Charlie and Roach were awake.

"Did you hear Old Indian? He knows Dad," said Tim.

"That can't *be*. Your dad is dead," said Roach with a yawn. "But then, how come he knows about Mom? *Gram* don't even know where she is? He said she'll come back, like she promised. Someday. How would he *know* that? And Gram. I-I guess I ain't been very nice to her. Gram misses Lizbet. But I never seen Gram cry."

"Grown-ups are too old to cry," said Tim, glancing at Charlie now lying on his stomach and propped up on his elbows.

"That's not all true. Mostly, grown-ups don't cry. But I seen Momma cry, and you seen your poppa cry, Tomata Head," said Charlie.

Roach frowned at Charlie. "Tomata Head? Why did you call him that?"

Charlie yawned. "Oh." He sat up, rubbed his eyes, and stretched. "It's a long story,"

Roach squinted at the boys. "Do you have a name for me, too?"

Tim never dared call her anything else. "No. Do you want us to call you another name?"

Roach sat up, frowning. "You mean a made-up name? Why would I want some silly name that don't make sense? I have a good name. I like it fine. Just call me 'Roach.' Short for Roachelle."

"Okay. Got it. Roach, short for Roachelle," said Charlie.

"Yeah. Roach it is," said Tim, in agreement.

"A name mother give you," said a voice from the shadows of the wigwam.

The three friends turned with a start. They hadn't realized the Indian couple slept at the other end of the wigwam.

The couple approached the fire pit where the evening's firewood had evaporated to gray piles of delicate, three-dimensional shapes of what used to be. Siômo left and soon returned with more firewood to rekindle the flame. She stirred the hot coals and arranged a handful of dried grass and dry firewood to help catch the remaining heat from the embers. Once the fire ignited and established a consistent flame, she turned to her guests and motioned that they follow.

Outside, she assigned chores for each of them to help prepare breakfast. They took turns stirring ground dried corn with water into a dough in a large wooden bowl, and flattening the thick mixture into several round, hand-sized shapes on a large, flat stone. Siômo placed the flattened dough on another hot flat stone sitting in the fire pit.

"Looks like pancakes. Is that what we're making?" asked Tim.

"Nope, we're making flatbread," said Charlie.

"They don't look like Mom's bread—big and puffy."

"No. Like I said, flatbread. Flat. You'll see. Tastes pretty good too."

"How do you know that?"

"Grampa used to make it. Had some more'n once."

Next, they boiled ground corn in more water until it looked like porridge. From a larger pouch, Siômo deposited a handful of sweet, chewy, dried berries into the mixture. She made tea in a clay bowl, with special plant leaves and a few dried roots from other nearby plants. Everyone got a portion of flatbread, porridge, and tea.

Roach stared at her serving for a few seconds, ripped a piece of flatbread, scooped her porridge, and placed it into her mouth. However, the piece was too large. Unable to keep her mouth closed, she covered her mouth with her hand, for she couldn't help drooling as she chewed.

Noticing her dilemma, the boys lowered their heads and stared at their porridge, stifling their urge to giggle.

Roach swallowed, drank her tea, and smiled when she noticed the boys had followed her example—scooping porridge with a piece of flatbread.

A second serving of tea completed the meal.

Tim liked its flavor. "That was a great breakfast Ma'am. And the tea tastes better than Kool-Aid. What do you think, Charlie?"

Charlie smirked at Tim and turned to Siômo. "The breakfast tasted mighty fine. Thank you Ma'am. Old Indian, sir, thank you."

"Yes. It was a delicious breakfast," said Roach. "Thank you."

After the meal, the guests learned to wash their bowls in the river with hands, fingers, knuckles, and fine gravel. Once the dishes and cooking stones were rinsed in the river's current, they were stacked in a pile to dry.

Tim imagined Mom's usual stack of fluffy blueberry pancakes topped with melting butter and golden maple syrup waiting for him. Although his stomach was full, his mouth watered for her cooking. And he missed her.

When would they get back home? Yes, it was nice here. Definitely better than being stuck in the cave. However, Tim had to tell Charlie about his experience in the wigwam without Roach hanging around.

After breakfast chores, the boys walked upriver to retrieve their shirts from their drying bush.

"What's Roach up to with them moccasins last night?" said Tim.

Charlie shook his head and shrugged his shoulders. "How would I know?"

"You blushed yesterday! Thought you couldn't do that 'cause you're black."

"It got hot, is all. I *can't* blush."

"No, it didn't, and yes you *can*. I was there. You like her?"

"She's just a kid." Charlie glared at Tim.

"She's about your age," said Tim, tilting his head, mimicking the glare back at Charlie.

"Is she?"

"Does it matter how old she is?"

"Yes. No. I mean, it's just not good," Charlie jambed his fists into his pockets.

"What do you mean? Is she too young or too old?"

Charlie stopped and faced Tim. "That ain't the point."

Tim stopped in turn, and raised his hands, palm up. "What's the point?"

"Like I said, it's just not good. She's...white."

"I'm white. I don't understand."

"She's annoying. And nice. And bossy. Does things without thinking."

"But that's who she is."

"She always like that?" Charlie pulled his hands out, placing them on his hips.

"Mostly," said Tim with a chuckle.

The boys arrived at the river and their drying bush.

"Well, like I said, Roach and me, it's not good to even think it. And I don't want to talk about it." Charlie yanked off his deerskin shirt and suddenly slapped it to the ground. Seconds later, he picked it up and sat on the river's edge, facing the river, where he carefully brushed off the shirt and folded it.

"Sorry, Tim. I-I got angry just then. We'll talk about it, sometime."

Tim sat next to Charlie. "Are you angry at me?"

"Huh? No. I'm not angry at *anyone*! It's just *me*."

Tim pondered what Charlie said. "I woke up thinking about Salubrious Frog this morning. He said *I* was angry. *Maybe* I am. But not at Dad or Mom. And not at God. I don't think I'm angry at Uncle Sal, even though he stopped me from reaching the ambulance last summer. Can-can someone be angry at their own...*self*?"

"Sure. You just seen it happen. I just got angry at no one but me." Charlie got up and retrieved clean shirt.

"You know, sometimes I feel that way, too. And I don't know why. Listen, I need to tell you what happened yesterday before Roach shows up." Tim glanced around, assuring himself of her absence.

"I'm listening," said Charlie, buttoning his shirt.

Tim described his experience about the hawk, the forest inside the wigwam, and the logger's accident.

"It was a terrible accident. I tried to help him, I yelled for you to come help. But you didn't answer. Then the other logger carried him away."

"Did you ever dream this before?"

Tim walked to the bush and retrieved his Kool-Aid stained shirt. He gave it a grimace, then slipped it on.

"I wasn't dreaming. It was real. I couldn't reach the man to save him. It was kinda like my dream where I swam one way but got dragged in the opposite direction.

"When the forest disappeared, the hawk flew back, coming at me really fast. Its eyes stared into mine, and it nearly hit me in the head."

"You had a vision. Your poppa came to help you because you didn't believe Old Indian. He came back just like when Poppa visited me, calling me downstairs with his cough and the fire in the wood stove. Just so we could be together one more time. That's how I see it."

Tim eyebrows met as he considered what Charlie said.

"You ever feel bad, or guilty—about your poppa dying?" asked Charlie.

"Guilty?"

"Yeah. Like, 'If I did this, or done that, he'd still be alive today.' Stuff like that?" said Charlie.

Tim's face blanched. He coughed, and with a squeak he said, "Yeah. I-I have."

"You never talked about it."

"I didn't realize it until just now, when you asked. I guess I been angry. *And* guilty that he died without me being there."

"You mean when your uncle stopped you?"

"No!" Tim burst into tears. "Dad planned to have me help him cut firewood. I wriggled my way out to-to dig up worms instead. I should have gone with him. He'd be *here* today!

"And I'm angry because I didn't ask enough questions to find the bear. I didn't ask Mom why I had to go to Gram's. Why didn't I? I always asked questions before. But when it was really important, I didn't. And it cost me *Dad!*"

His head down, Tim crossed his arms and clutched his shoulders. "I know his spirit is supposed to be with me. But I want him back, not just his spirit. I want *all* of him!"

"That hawk focused on you at your poppa's lean-to, remember? Maybe it wanted to calm you when you were sad, trying not to cry. And when you made eye contact inside the wigwam, maybe it wanted you to look hard into your soul.

"First you wanted to blame other people; be angry at them. Now, you're angry at yourself because you didn't do what you think you should'a done. It's easier to blame someone else than it is to forgive yourself. I know. I been there," said Charlie.

"You think so? But why did I see that horrible accident?"

"Could be that was your poppa with the chainsaw. The hawk showed you there was nothing you could do. Was the other man Uncle Sal?"

"I focused on the bleeding logger. I'm not sure. It could have been Uncle Sal. He tried to save Dad.

"Nothing I could do either to rescue that logger—rescue Dad. It must 'a been too late."

"If it was your uncle, then you see, even he couldn't help save your poppa.

"*He* must feel awful! Maybe that's why you two have a hard time together. He feels guilty, and when he stopped you from catching up with the ambulance—

"Man, that must have been hard on everyone!"

Tim rubbed his eyes with his palms and took a deep breath. Controlling an urge to cry, Tim's voice cracked a little. "And Mom— Mom didn't want me to see the blood. That must be why she locked the screen door; why she kept rubbing her hands up and down her apron. Maybe her hands were all bloodied from Dad's accident.

"And Uncle Sal, stopping me from reaching the ambulance—

"I understand now. But I wish I had seen Dad, talked to him, told him I loved him. Hugged him one last time!"

Charlie rubbed Tim's back. "You *saw* him. In your vision. Your poppa gave you that vision so you could forgive yourself. He knows you're grown-up enough to understand what you saw. Even if it was awful, he wanted you to know it wasn't your fault he died. Great Spirit decided. It was time for your poppa to leave the land. But his spirit will be with you. *Forever*."

The boys sat quietly, each reflecting on the events since leaving for their overnight camp-out.

Before he left for the camp-out, Tim was just a kid. Today he felt grown up. He inhaled a deep breath, released it in a puff, and shook his head side to side slowly.

Wearing their own dry, fresh-smelling cotton shirts and their new moccasins, they returned their borrowed clothing to Siômo. "Thank you, Ma'am, for letting us wear these." She took the clothes and smiled, nodding at the boys.

"You be home soon," said Old Indian.

"We will?" said Tim.

"Ponômuk. Come." Old Indian patted the earth near where he sat. Tim noticed the large, gnarled hands. The skin, dry and rough; two fingers twisted at the joints, their knuckles larger than the others. They were ancient hands. Strong hands.

Once seated, Tim blurted, "Tell me what you talk about, Sir. With Dad."

"You speak to me, you speak to him. We are one. Same. Great Spirit be with your father. Your father be with you. Great Spirit be with all people."

"Will Dad always be with me?"

"Oho. Yes. His spirit be with you. His spirit listen to you. Talk to you."

"Can I *see* Dad's spirit?"

"Not everyone see spirit. If you have good heart, maybe you see."

"What does a spirit look like?" asked Tim.

"Many things look like spirit. Spirit is bird, animal, dream. Spirit walk in sun, fire, rain. You see. Listen. You will know."

"Spirit walk in fire? Like in a fire pit. Like this one?"

Old Indian nodded.

Tim's heart skipped a beat. *It's true; I saw Dad. Charlie was right about the vision.*

"Is Dad with Mom, too?"

"Yes. He speak to her."

"If he speaks to me, will he talk out loud?"

"You will hear him in your heart."

"In my heart? How will I know what he said?"

The Indian placed his arm across his chest. "You listen here. Inside. In your heart. You will know. You will know."

Tim nodded. He had heard Dad. No one else heard him. No one else saw. He understood it in his head, but there was no sound. So it must have come from his heart.

Dad misses me like I miss him. That's why he came back! That's what happened. He walked in the fire pit. He spoke to me from the fire!

Just then, Tim realized Old Indian knew what he was thinking. He knew Dad visited yesterday! Tim smiled at Old Indian.

The Indian nodded in return.

Tim did all he could to find Dad. And he *found* him! He'd tell Mom as soon as he got home.

Everything will be fine. Right, Dad?

That one thought made him feel good. He was talking to Dad, not crying or whining. Just talking to him like he was *there*. Tim smiled. He was alone, yet unafraid. He had moved away from the darkness into the light.

In a whisper, Roach asked Old Indian, "My mom, Lizbet Hallstead, where is she? Will she come for me?"

Old Indian placed his right hand over his heart, nodding to Roach. "Mother not come today, not come many days. Speak to Great Spirit. Great Spirit will hear. He will speak to you. Listen with your heart."

Roach stroked her mother's necklace and closed her eyes.

Charlie wiped a tear from his cheek. The Indian nodded at him. Charlie nodded back. "I know you're here, Poppa," he whispered.

Quiet surrounded the three friends as they each focused on their missing parent.

Old Indian's announcement startled them back to the present. "We go now. Ponômuk. We go in canoe to your home—to your people."

Chapter 35

I AM ABENAKI

O N LAND, HIS FEET were sure and swift. On the river, Old Indian guided his canoe with mastery. Within minutes, they were in a familiar place.

"Charlie, Roach. We're near the cave. We're on the Saco," said Tim.

Charlie frowned, shaking his head. "Wow! Just like that? How can that be? We started out maybe less than five minutes ago."

They witnessed the destruction caused by the storm. Tim shivered at the thought that things could have turned out worse for him and his friends. Wildlife appeared to have accepted the changed environment and had returned to the daily routines. Tim's campsite came into view with Dad's lean-to gone.

The large hemlock's missing top floated near the cave's entrance. Staring at the standing remains of the hemlock still camouflaging the cave's opening, Tim whispered, "Be back later for your lunchbox, Dad."

He turned to Charlie. "Four days ago, the storm trapped us in that cave and now we're free! We're going home! And we *saw* Tiny Bear."

Then he whispered to Charlie, "I talked to Old Indian about the bear, but I never asked if he *knew* Tiny Bear."

"Who's Tiny Bear?" asked Roach.

Annoyed she overheard, Tim said, "Ah— He's the tiniest bear in the world. Dad told me about him."

"Is your dad talking to you now? Why is he telling you stuff like that about a bear?" asked Roach.

"No. Before he die—" Tim coughed to loosen the tightness in his throat.

"Sorry, Tim, I didn't mean to make you sad," said Roach, stroking his shoulder.

"No. It's-it's okay. Dad...died. I have to accept that. Before he died, he told me about Tiny Bear. It rescued Dad and Uncle Sal when they were boys."

"They heard the bear laugh, and it rescued them," added Charlie with a slight grin.

"Laugh? A laughing bear?" said Roach, turning to Tim with a what-are-you-talking-about stare. "Who ever heard of a laughing bear?"

Charlie winked at Tim. Then he poked Tim's arm, leaned over and whispered, "We gotta thank the couple for helping us. Do you remember Old Indian's name?"

"I think it's...Teezee Whatsis? But it don't sound right. He said to call him 'Old Indian.'"

"I am Tsi'-dzis Awasos," said Old Indian.

"Yeah, that's it," said Tim.

Surprised he had overheard, the three friends chorused, "Thank you, Tsi'-dzis Awasos."

"Thank you for rescuing and helping us go back home," said Tim.

Charlie adapted a new sing-a-long on the spot:

"Row, row, row your canoe
Tsi'-dzis Awasos, thank you.
Paddle, paddle down the stream
This is not a dream."

His friends joined in. Roach sang the loudest, if not better than the boys.

"You have a different name like me," said Roach. "I like my name and I like yours too, Tsi'-dzis Awasos."

"Roachelle. Name make Mother proud. Roachelle proud," said Tsi'-dzis Awasos with a smile.

Roach beamed at Tsi'-dzis Awasos, then at Charlie. This time he returned her smile, and her face warmed to a shade of pink. His face flushed in a pinkish glow as they held their gaze for several seconds. And he didn't look away.

"Where do you come from, Tsi'-dzis Awasos?" asked Tim.

"I walked this land many winters ago. I am Abenaki. We are Pequawket from Abenaki tribe. My people cross many rivers to this land. Now your people walk this land. But when friend need help, I come. I help. Then I return to my people."

"Is your wife's name Mrs. Awasos? Does she always come with you?" asked Roach.

"My wife be Makazawigek Siômo. She be with me."

"You said 'friend', are we your friends?" asked Tim.

Tsi'-dzis Awasos gave a solemn nod.

Tim smiled in return.

The canoe reached shallow water in the Lower Wood, and Tsi'-dzis Awasos stepped out, pulled the canoe aground, steadying it with one hand, helping the three passengers step out with his other hand. The friends hurried up the Lower Wood's mangled, yet still familiar path, leading to the Old Wood, bound for home. Tsi'-dzis Awasos followed close behind.

Once they arrived at the edge of the Old Wood, they stood at the end of the field that separated the forest from Tim's farm. All cheered, hollered and squealed at finding Nel, Lila, Uncle Sal, and Gram.

Uncle Sal stood talking with the sheriff. The deputy sheriff wrote in a notebook with Nel and Lila who, with hands clasped, studied the notes being taken. Gram leaned against Ol' Elroy. Her truck was obviously stuck and parked at a tipped angle in the muddy field. Other cars and trucks were parked in the driveway. People had gathered in three groups with ropes, flashlights, and blankets strewn on the hoods of their vehicles. Each group had one person talking and pointing toward the Old Wood as the others listened.

While the friends observed the scene at Tim's farm, a deep laugh echoed from behind. Turning to investigate, they found Tsi'-dzis Awasos had vanished, and a black hawk circled high above the trees before it swerved back into the Old Wood and disappeared, heading toward the river.

Chapter 36

THE REUNION

"TIM!" CALLED NEL WITH a shriek, running with arms out-stretched toward the three friends. Lila and Uncle Sal quickly followed. Gram slumped down on Ol' Elroy's running board. Reaching out, she exclaimed, "Roachelle!"

The officers raced ahead. The other people stayed put, observing.

"You kids okay? Anybody hurt?" said one sheriff.

"We're okay Mr. Sheriff," said Tim.

"Yesterday, after the storm, your Uncle Sal called and we searched for you all day. You been missing a whole day! We were just getting ready this morning to search again with a group of River Fork volunteers," said the sheriff.

"One day? Just one? Felt like more'n a day to me," said Tim.

The second sheriff chuckled. "When scary things happen, hours seem pretty long 'fore you get help." He took a quick survey of the friends' physical condition. All seemed fine. He smiled. "Glad to have you back." He nodded his head, extended his arm and open hand in a swoop toward the farm and let them pass.

The three friends chorused, "Mom!" "Momma!" "Gram!"

Mothers and sons connected, and the boys nearly suffocated with hugs and kisses. Tears flowed freely. Roach and Gram sat in a tight embrace on Ol' Elroy's running board.

"I'm sorry, Gram," said Roach.

"I'm sorry too, child," whispered Gram, cupping Roachelle's face in her hands. Their foreheads touched, and both of them laughed and cried at the same time.

Uncle Sal blotted his tears with his shirtsleeve as they all marched to Nel's and waved to the neighbors who cheered their approach.

Lila, Nel, and Sal, and the three friends, hugged, shook hands, and thanked the volunteers for their offer of help. Uncle Sal stayed outside with the Sheriff to answer more questions and to talk with the volunteers.

Once inside, Nel noticed the footwear. "Where did you three get those moccasins?"

"Roach made them," said Tim.

"She did? My, my! Isn't she talented! They are lovely! But where are your shoes?"

"In the cave. We got trapped in the cave, Mom."

"How were you trapped?"

"The river flooded it, but Charlie and I found a high up shelf and we stayed there."

"Oh my. I'm happy you made it back. Charlie, thank you. Thank you for taking care of Tim." Nel hugged Charlie.

"Was Roach with you?" asked Gram.

"No. We don't know where she was," said Charlie, frowning, facing Roach.

"Where were you? Where did you get that Indian dress? And where did you learn to make moccasins?" asked Gram.

"I got lost." Roach looked down at her feet, her hands smoothing the sides of the leather dress. "I don't remember about the dress. Or the moccasins. Where are my shoes? My clothes?"

"Charlie, what happened?" asked Lila.

"Like Tim said, we got stuck in a cave, Momma."

"So, how did you get back? Tim's uncle rowed his boat up and down the river near the campsite, searching for you boys."

"He did? I have to thank Uncle Sal," said Tim.

Charlie puzzled at what had happened? "We got out. Somehow. I don't remember." Still frowning, he said, "Roach, how'd you get here dressed like that? If you made these moccasins, and you weren't with us, how'd we get 'em?"

"Don't...know." Roach shook her head, pondering the events from the time she followed the boys. "I worried I wouldn't get back, Gram. I needed to get back 'cause I was sorry about the cat. It got dark so fast. I heard the wolf howl, and the storm happened. Then the shadow-man told me Mom's coming to get me someday. You know she'll come back, don't you?"

"What wolf? The shadow-man? My Lizbet— I don't know— Ah, yes. She will, someday. Lizbet will come back soon as she can. We'll see...we'll see." said Gram with a sad smile and a tremble in her voice.

"Mom, do you know Dad is always with us?" asked Tim.

Startled by the question, Nel gazed out the window toward the Old Wood. After a few moments, she hugged Tim, whispering in his ear, "Dad is always with us. Listen with your heart and you'll hear him. I hear him when I listen."

"That's what Old Indian said."

"Who's Old Indian?" chorused Lila, Nel, and Gram.

"I-I don't know. But someone—an Indian—said Dad is with us. He said we can talk to Dad, and Dad can talk to us," said Tim.

"Nel, maybe we can talk about this later," said Gram. "I'm plum wore out. Roach looks tired. We need to rest for a spell. Thank you all for your help. I couldn't a done it without you. You're all wonderful neighbors. Come, Roachelle."

"Ponômuk," said Roachelle.

"What?" said Gram.

"Ponômuk, means 'come.' Ponômuk, Gram." Roach took Gram's hand, leading her to the door.

"Where did you learn that?" said Gram.

Roach shrugged.

"Say 'thank you' to our friends," said Gram.

"Thank you. Will I see you tomorrow, Charlie?" asked Roach.

Charlie frowned and said nothing.

"Roachelle," said Lila, "you and Tim can visit any time. We'll be happy to see the both of you."

"Thank you, Mrs. Wallace." Roach smiled at her, but Tim's inclusion in the invitation disappointed Roach. He was such a nosy busybody!

"Everyone! Come for breakfast tomorrow morning around 8:30. We'll chat over pancakes and hot chocolate. The children look tired. We'll let them rest."

All agreed to return the next morning.

Once the sheriff filled out his report, he borrowed a logging chain from one of the volunteers, knocked at the kitchen door, and announced he and his deputy were leaving, but first, they and Uncle Sal would pull Ol' Elroy out of the mud."

Uncle Sal stepped up behind the Sheriff and smiled. "Happy to oblige."

Within half an hour, Old Elroy, Gram, and Roach were on their way home.

Chapter 37

HOME

Mom kissed Tim goodnight, wished him a good night's sleep, gave him a hug, left the room, and shut his bedroom door behind her.

"Thanks, Dad, for being here with me and Mom," Tim whispered.

Was Dad telling him to be careful of the Saco in that awful dream he kept having? If so, he'd been with Tim the whole time.

Tim got out of bed, went to the window, and pulled his shade halfway up. He looked out to the dark sky, the twinkling stars, the moon, and the Old Wood.

"Sorry I left your lunchbox in the cave."

The cave, I remember. But how did we get back home? How come Roach just showed up?

He pulled the shade down for the night, nestled back under the sheet and, as he drifted into sleep, he sensed a presence nearby. He knew it wasn't a ghost. Had to be Dad. And he wasn't scared at being alone in his room with the lights out. Tomorrow, he'd open that attic door and check for the mouse, catch it and bring it to the woods to live with other mice. But would it stay? Well, maybe he'd let it remain in the attic, like an old friend, like family. Why send it away?

Tim suddenly felt it, or did he hear it, in his heart? "I love you Tim."

Tim replied, "I love you too, Dad." And he fell into a deep, peaceful sleep.

To celebrate his return, Momma served Charlie his favorite meal. Meatloaf, mashed potatoes, Kool-Aid, and apple pie. After giving Momma a hug, he climbed up to his room and sat on his bed.

How come we came back home with Roach?

His cheeks grew warm. What was wrong? Did he have a fever? He went to the mirror. His face *was* kinda rosy? A little like Tim. He thought of Roach in her new dress. His cheeks got rosier.

He smiled for a moment, shook his head, and returned to his bed confused about all that happened since he and Tim left for their overnight camp-out.

Charlie mulled over his efforts to escape from the flooded cave. The flood— He nearly drowned! Yet he survived! But he can't swim. Weren't they gone for about four days? But the sheriff said one day. That they returned the second day.

Events appeared in a jumble in his brain. Maybe when he slept, Poppa would tell him what he needed to know.

Charlie closed his eyes and lay back on his pillow. Although very sleepy, his mind wandered.

How did we get home? How'd I get moccasins? Roach made them? But she wasn't with us.

Roach has green eyes. Or are they hazel? The color reminds me of copper.

Charlie hummed and mumbled in his half sleep.

"Row, row, row your canoe
Tsi'-dzis...thank you.

...the stream
...not...dream."
He fell asleep and snored.

—*ell*—

Funnyface greeted Gram and Roach with a loud "Meow!" Roach picked him up, hugged him, let him rub his head at her neck and lick her ear. "I'm so sorry I kicked you the other day. I didn't mean it. It was an accident."

To make it up to Funnyface, Roach poured him a large dish of milk. Funnyface purred; walked around Roach's feet with his tail quivering, wrapping itself around her leg; happy she was home again.

Once in her room, Roach placed the deerskin dress and moccasins on her bedroom chair.

How did she get that dress and those moccasins? Where were her clothes? She absolutely *didn't* know how to make moccasins!

Why do these things happen to me?

She Climbed into bed and snuggled under her summer quilt blanket. "I'm so happy to be in my soft comfortable bed again." Her head sank into her fluffy feather pillow, and she fell asleep.

She dreamed about a black hawk flying overhead as she ran through the Magic Meadow with Funnyface running ahead. They ran toward a woman wearing a red necklace. Charlie kept pace alongside, smiling, wearing moccasins especially made for him.

Roach smiled in her sleep as Funnyface slept, purring on her other pillow.

Chapter 38

THE MUSTACHE

Tim awakened in a darkened bedroom to the rooster's early sunrise crowing. And he hadn't once covered his head during the night like he usually did—to hide from ghosts. "J. J. Jones can keep his ghosts, monsters, and vampires. They aren't real," said Tim.

Back to his familiar surroundings, Tim heard the mouse scamper above his bedroom. "Thanks for being there for me, buddy," said Tim with a smile.

Sprawled in his bed, he remembered, "According to the sheriff, this is the *third* day after the hurricane. So it's July 19. We got back in time for my *birthday*. I'm thirteen! I'm *not* a little kid anymore!"

He turned to the alarm clock. It had stopped working after it crashed under the bed. Perhaps Uncle Sal could fix it. Picking it up, he noticed a ticking sound. It worked? The time seemed about right. But last he knew, it got busted.

Who fixed it? Then he remembered he had asked Dad to fix it when they came back home. That was it!

"Dad's home!" he said aloud.

He fell back against his pillow, hugging the clock. "Thanks for the Birthday present, Dad." He smiled at the window shade as the light peeked around the edges.

A sudden puff of wind blew through the open window into the room, pulling at the shade, which suddenly rolled upward with a snap.

Tim promptly sat up.

"That happened before! That was Dad then! That morning when the shade flipped off its brackets in the window and knocked the alarm clock off the night stand. That was Dad! And Dad was with me at the cemetery. And he's with me now. I can *feel* him!

"Hi Dad. Glad you came for my Birthday."

Tim smiled and wiped a tear trickling down his cheek. He lay back into his pillow until he heard Mom stepping down the stairway, making her way to the kitchen.

Hopping out of bed, Tim retrieved a crayon from his bureau drawer and opened his closet door. He stepped back against the door-jamb, pressing his shoulders and head against the jamb, and with the crayon flat at the top of his head, he marked a fresh line. Crossing his fingers, he turned to see the mark and, with a ruler, measured the distance from the previous mark.

"I did it! I grew two inches in the last two months!"

Once dressed, he ran downstairs and joined Mom in the kitchen.

"Happy Birthday, Sweetie. Uncle Sal is coming for breakfast along with the others. Want to help set the table?"

"Sure. Mom, I just measured myself. I grew two inches!"

"Oh, are you happy about that?"

"I sure am."

"Well, then I'm happy, too."

Tim gathered the silverware from the kitchen table's drawer, placed it in a pile on the table, paused, and sat in Dad's rocking chair, frowning.

"What's wrong Tim?"

"I'll miss this place. Why do we have to move? Everything about Dad is here. All those memories. All his things: the swing, his hat still hanging on that hook next to the stove. Can't we stay here in River Fork?"

Reaching for the measuring cup, Mom's eyes wandered to the hat. She clutched the measuring cup and pressed it hard against her stomach.

"Mom, you okay?" said Tim.

In silence, she placed the cup on the counter, wiped her hands, sat at the table near Tim, and took a quick breath. "You heard me talking with Uncle Sal about moving?"

"Yeah. I don't want to move. It ain't fair to move...leaving Dad alone in the cemetery."

"Wouldn't you be happier away from all this? The memory of Dad dying. The chores. Being far from your friends, far from school?"

"In Boston, you would be close to everything. I'd get a job to pay for an apartment."

"Can't we just move in with Uncle Sal? He has a big house. It would be easier for you there."

Mom tilted her head, frowning at Tim. "Uncle Sal's farm? I couldn't do that. Uncle Sal's a bachelor because he likes it that way. We would be an imposition.

"Seeing how sad you were, Uncle Sal and I thought you would be happier being closer to school friends. And not having to do chores around the farm. You could focus on school instead of the farm. Were we wrong?"

"Yeah. You were both wrong. I been here all my life. Thirteen years is a long time! I love it here. I don't want to leave. Do you?"

Mom half smiled. A tear suddenly trickled down her cheek. She quickly stood, wiped her cheek with her hand, and with her head down, she walked to the sink.

"Mom, I'm sorry if I made you cry."

Shaking her head, she faced Tim with a frown. "No. No Tim. *You* didn't make me cry. I been holding it in for too long. I didn't want to upset you. Grown-ups aren't supposed to cry, you know. But that's silly. Life isn't always fair. We end up crying once in a while. When something bad happens, we cry. Then we have to deal with it. And we go on. It's okay to cry, even if it hurts. It's normal. Eventually, you get back to living and doing what needs doing. What you have left are memories. The good *and* the bad."

"Just like the river. Peaceful and happy, then stormy and destructive...and peaceful again," said Tim.

"You've grown up a lot since a year ago. And we haven't talked about how *you* feel. How *I* feel. *We'll* have to fix that. Okay?" said Mom.

Tim's eyes grew bleary with the threat of tears. "I'd like that. I miss Dad. Talking about him would be good for both of us."

Mom wiped her eyes, nodding yes. Kneeling at Tim's side, she hugged him and whispered, "Let's give it another try. Okay?"

Tim smiled wide. "Okay. We'll do better this time. I promise."

"You making flatbread?" asked Tim.

"Flatbread? What makes you ask? You never had flatbread," said Mom.

"Don't know. It popped in my head. An Indian lady made some for us."

"What Indian lady?"

"Tsi'-dzis Awasos's wife, Makazawigek Siômo, made flatbread for me, Charlie and Roach."

"Roachelle? Tim, she was with you? Do you remember anything else?"

Tim frowned, leaning forward in the rocking chair. "Nope. But I just said she was, didn't I? I don't understand."

"It's okay. Do you remember anything else?"

"About what?"

"About how you escaped from the cave."

After a lengthy pause, Tim answered, "No. Sorry, Mom."

A familiar-sounding truck pulled up, followed by a knock at the porch door.

"Answer the door for me," said Mom.

Tim ran to the door, let Uncle Sal in, and accepted his firm hug. He didn't seem serious or grumpy like before. Perhaps he liked Tim after all.

Uncle Sal walked into the kitchen.

Was there something in his jacket?

There was a definite bulge in his jacket.

"Morning, Nel. Tim. My, it sure smells good in here."

"Morning to you, Sal. Pour yourself a coffee. Have a seat. The others will be here soon. Tim just remembered something interesting."

"Oh? What was that?" Uncle Sal poured a cup of coffee and stepped to the table.

"Tell Uncle Sal about the flatbread."

"Yeah. Makazawigek Siômo made flatbread for me, Charlie, and Roach. She's Tsi'-dzis Awasos's wife."

Uncle Sal turned to Tim with a blank expression. All color drained from his face. "Oh, my goodness. They came back!" His free hand clutched the table, and he nearly missed the chair.

Nel and Tim, both surprised and concerned at Uncle Sal's stumbling, asked in unison, "Who?"

As he sat, Uncle Sal's usual color returned.

"Tim. Nel. You remember Wes believed in Tiny Bear?"

"Yeah! And I do too," said Tim, eyes wide and smiling.

"Tim, Tsi'-dzis Awasos is Abenaki for Tiny Bear and Makazawigek Siômo means Black Hawk."

Now Tim's face blanched and slowly returned to its usual shade of freckle-red. Although dumbfounded, images came back to him: Tsi'-dzis Awasos appearing in the cave. A black hawk circling Dad's lean-to. The hawk coming at him inside the wigwam. The hawk flying back into the Old Wood after Tsi'-dzis Awasos laughed and disappeared from behind him, Charlie and Roach.

"Mom! Uncle Sal! Tiny Bear is real! He rescued me, Charlie and Roach. Dad told me to believe in Tiny Bear. I do. And Dad came back in a vision. He told me he loved me. That he'd always be with me.

Nel leaned against the counter, wiping tears from her cheeks with her apron. With tears welling in his eyes, Uncle Sal gave Tim a broad smile, grabbed a hand from both Nel and Tim, and squeezed them firmly in his own. For Tim that was a symbol. It connected them like a chain. A family chain.

Once they let go, Tim noticed Uncle Sal wipe a tear from his eye as he stirred his coffee. Mom returned to the stove to check the pancakes. All three were stunned and quiet.

After they settled, Tim couldn't ignore the bulge in his uncle's jacket any longer. "What you got, Uncle Sal?"

"Ah, you noticed!" Uncle Sal's voice had become a little thin. He cleared his throat, sniffed, and tapped the bulge. "Well, it *is* your birthday." He looked at Tim with a smile. "*I* brought *you* a present." His voice returned to its usual firm tone. "A book about giant frogs. I noticed you looking at it during your last two visits and thought you'd like a copy. So, I went to North Conway and found one for you.

"That's where I got stranded during the hurricane. The road got washed out and I couldn't make it back. And that's why I didn't come check on you. I'm so sorry, Tim."

"That's okay, Uncle Sal."

"The title is Brobdingnagian Frogs, by Professor John Salubrious. Here, it's yours. Happy Birthday, Tim. 'Brobdingnagian' means gigantic."

"Salubrious? Gigantic? Salubrious Frog! So that's where that comes from. Thank you, Uncle Sal. Thank you.

"Mom, can I go to Charlie's? I gotta show him. Mom?" Tim's speech was quick and breathless with excitement. And it cracked, just a little.

Both Sal and Nel wondered what Tim was up to. Why was he so animated over a book about frogs?

"May I?" said Mom.

"Oh, yeah. May I, Mom?"

"My oh my, Tim. Aren't you excited this morning? Remember, everyone will be here pretty soon. But, okay, go along now to Charlie's, and tell them we're waiting for them and they better be hungry. Go and-and be careful. Come, give me a kiss and a hug, and give Uncle Sal a hug for his present."

Tim hugged and kissed his mom. He gave a quick hug to his uncle and noticed his coal-black eyes, his bushy eyebrows, and mustache.

"Uncle Sal, did you know your eyebrows look like your mustache got sneezed up your face?"

Tim's face and ears burned hot with embarrassment. He immediately looked down to his new book.

I can't believe I just said that!

For a moment, all were quiet, then Uncle Sal burst into laughter. Tears sparkled, trickling from his coal-black eyes, and his face grew red. Mom laughed with Sal. Tim didn't know what to do other than laugh, too.

"You are a treat! You're just like my brother, Wes!" said Uncle Sal with difficulty through his laughing fit.

"I am? You think so?"

"Absolutely!"

"Gee, thanks, Uncle Sal."

Tim ran out the door to share his book with Charlie. He had to tell him Tiny Bear was *real*. That the bear had rescued him, Charlie and Roach. And helped Tim find Dad!

Oho! Yes!

He really did!

The End

Glossary

Abenaki Language

Below, Abenaki words are translated to English.

The Abenaki alphabet includes an '8', as a nasal 'n' sound.

Aa Bb Cc Dd Ee Gg Hh Ii Jj Kk Ll Mm Nn Oo 8 Pp Ss Tt Uu Ww Zz

(To avoid confusion, this story's narrative replaced the '8' with the 'n'.)

agukimômuk - teach

ahamo+ak - chicken

awôssis - young child

idôzik (or) ida - say

kadosmimek - drink

kassi - so many, so much

kchi - great

Kchi Niwaskw - Great Spirit

kigawes - your mother

kiuwô - you

k'mitôgwes - your father

nidoba agema - he is my friend

kzôbo - soup

majekisgad kwelbiwi - bad weather behind

manna8ékkañn - lost boys
mkezen+al - moccasin
nda - no
nda sagzimek - no fear
nda Kigawes - no mother
nia - I
n'ôkskuasis - young girl
n'ôkskuasis kazebaalmuk - young girl wash
nokmes - Grandmother
nolka+k - deer
oho (or) ôhôô - yes
Pegwaket - North Conway Abenaki Band
ponômuk - come
poskwezômuk - cut with knife
Sawascotuck - outflowing, Saco River
taôlawi - like
tapsedawômuk - listen to
w'skinnossis - our little boy
wigewessa - her mother

Learn More About the Abenaki Indians
• https://westernabenaki.com/pronunciation.php
• https://en.wikipedia.org/wiki/Abenaki_language
New Hampshire Abenaki natives spoke the Algonquin Indian Nation's language. The same word is often spelled differently from tribe to tribe. The Abenaki tribe, as well as other Indian nations, often understood each other because the words were similar.

Their language may still be familiar to us today.

Acknowledgements

River Fork: <u>The Bear in the Storm</u> and its sequel, <u>Roach and the Wolves</u>, came about from years of just writing what was in my head.

Then the hard work began—how to write a novel. My tenacious attitude, along with the encouragement of family, friends, and colleagues helped me learn and plod on through this long writing journey.

Tom, my husband, encouraged me to follow my heart's desire—to not only paint, but to write. He reviewed chapter upon chapter as I slogged through the first draft of <u>River Fork: The Bear in the Storm</u>.

Meredith West, writer and book lover; and C. T. Charles, author, introduced this newbie writer to the artful process of writing. Judy Brody, a book lover, did the very first beta read of my raw manuscript.

After many edits, Shauna Alderson, a Canadian author, gave me the real lowdown. She pointed out segments where I needed to rethink my story! Jessica Nelson, author, pointed to similar issues and provided links to resources which helped clarify some principles I had not understood.

Much later, Amy Sumner-McCluney, a book lover, provided a beta-read offering pointers. Later, M. J. Ellis, a writer, and teacher from Georgia, provided a critique. She was right on the mark. And her Southern heritage helped solidify the speech of my Southern characters. Judith Kammeraad, author, carefully reviewed my story, giving me further pointers about writing and encouraging me to publish my story. Mary Ellen Kelleher, an English Major, and a neighbor, reviewed my manuscript and pointed out errors, assumptions, and inconsistencies included in the narrative.

Finally, Mary Lu Scholl, author, reviewed my final draft, offered suggestions, and encouraged me to publish a story she felt teens and parents would enjoy and benefit from reading.

All those mentioned above helped me make important decisions: to add, cut, and re-work parts of my manuscript. They encouraged me to continue writing and to publish a story they said needed to be "put out there."

To all these people, I extend my heartfelt gratitude.

It was a challenging process, but completing my debut novel was incredibly rewarding. I loved it all—the research, the writing, the critiques, and the learning.

About the author

J. M. Orise, a Maine native, earned a BS degree in Art Education, with an Endorsement in Computer Science from the University of Maine, Gorham, ME. She later studied Children's Book Publishing and Illustration at the Portland School of Art (now known as Maine College of Art and Design), Portland, ME, where, for teacher certification renewal, she also studied creative storytelling and writing poetry.

Her twenty-year teaching career occurred mostly at the high school level, where she taught art, computer science, web design, desktop publishing, and introduced computer animation at Gorham, Wells, and Waterboro high schools. She finally taught at Portsmouth High School, Portsmouth, NH, where she introduced Internet Safety into the curriculum, assisted by the Portsmouth Internet Forensic Police Department.

Orise often writes poetry, which she stores in a briefcase. While at the Portland School of Art, she wrote a children's story based on an ancient tale, which she stored with her poems.

Being an artist, Orise considers writing as painting with words.

When not writing, you will find her at Orise Studio Gallery painting and teaching beginner and advanced art lessons.

Orise and her husband live in mid-coast Maine, as well as on Florida's Nature Coast, where they feed the crows who sit in the branches of a nearby tree, next to their patio, to chat with Orise.

https://jmorise.com/

Dear Reader,

Did you enjoy **River Fork: The Bear In the Storm**?

Look for the sequel, **River Fork: Roach and the Wolves,** where sixteen year old Roach deals with grief, coming of age, teen romance, humor, and Jim Crow laws with the same River Fork friends you have come to know.

Could I please ask you to help me continue writing by doing the following?

1. **Write one honest and brief review** wherever you purchased the book. (Reviews help sell books and encourage authors to continue writing.)

2. Tell your family and friends personally, or through your social media outlets.

3. Or, write and email your review to jm@jmorise.com. Sign your name and your review could be included in an updated version of the book!

This Author **thanks you,**
J. M. Orise